To Jim,
a small token for your
late-night-reading
June '93

# THE FINAL BOUNDARY

**By the same author:**

*Join the Company*
*The Sacred Diary of Adrian Plass*

# The Final Boundary

**ADRIAN PLASS**

**KINGSWAY PUBLICATIONS**
EASTBOURNE

ISBN 0 86065 523 7

*Cover illustration by James Hammond*

Printed in Great Britain for
KINGSWAY PUBLICATIONS LTD
Lottbridge Drove, Eastbourne, E. Sussex BN23 6NT by
Cox & Wyman Ltd, Reading.
Typeset by CST, Eastbourne, E. Sussex.

# Contents

To my mother,
whose life is the best modern parable I know.

# Preface

A parable is a story that entertains at the front door while the truth slips in through a side window. Having effected its entrance this truth may lie unnoticed for a long time, or you might trip over it as you close the door and turn around. It doesn't really matter how the discovery happens. It doesn't even matter if the story and the truth are never connected in the mind of the reader or listener. What is important is that the mind is distracted and the truth gets in.

The greatest ever exponent of this form of teaching dealt with a difficult Jewish audience two thousand years ago, and his parables (still widely published) have certain interesting things in common.

First, they were almost invariably secular in content (as opposed to meaning), and they were usually extremely lively. I am not yet spiritual enough to be that secular, but I have managed to avoid mention of God in most of these stories, and I have tried to make them lively.

Secondly, the master story-teller made sure that his narratives were rooted in culture and understanding of the people who heard them. Characters and events were always linked with contemporary, recognisable people and situations. Some readers have been puzzled by the inclusion in this book of stories such as 'Why It Was All Right to Kill Uncle Reginald'. This is a detailed account of a man's obsessional preoccupation with the way in which his uncle (a very normal eater) consumes his food. After ten years of mounting yet closely concealed repulsion, he decides that he is divinely ordained to execute his uncle, and proceeds to carry out the 'sentence' with a clear conscience.

Are these recognizable people in a recognizable situation? Well, a man in America was murdered by his flatmate recently for 'using too much toilet paper'. In Britain last year a little girl was tortured and starved to death because those who had charge of her allowed no external reference points to influence the distorted code of conduct that had developed from their private and particular little 'circle line' of perception. These are extreme cases. So was Nazism. So is the Ku-Klux Klan. So is apartheid. But the general principle holds good in many more familiar areas, albeit in a scaled down form. Home, church, relationships, whenever people retreat into an unmonitored and obsessively exclusive set of attitudes, habits or beliefs, there is the danger that someone will be hurt or rejected for the *best possible reasons*. Uncle Reginald is not a pleasant story. It is not meant to be.

A third feature of the parables of Jesus was their fictional nature. They were stories. They were made up. They were not true. I can't think of any other way of saying it. Each event in The Good Samaritan, for instance, needs to be seen in the context of the whole story and its overall intention. The fact that a man is beaten up and robbed and left for dead in the parable does not mean that Jesus is implicitly approving of such activities. Nor is he trying to say that priests, Levites, or anyone else for that matter, *should* pass by on the other side. There are necessary elements in a story which aims to teach the fundamental truth that your neighbour can be identified as being anyone who needs you, or who offers to help when you are needy. This may appear a rather naïvely obvious point, but I suspect that the acceptance of fiction in modern Christian literature depends upon an understanding of this particular aspect of the parable form. After all, the Bible itself describes scenes and events that are, in themselves, extremely distasteful (Lot's treatment of his daughters is one of many examples), but because the Christian sees these sections in the context of God's overall communication to his people, they continue to be part of the Good Book, a book which is, furthermore, available to Christians and non-Christians alike.

Hastily disassociating myself from any implied claim that my writings are on a par with Scripture, I do nevertheless make an impassioned plea that readers will look beyond the odd item that might cause offence and consider the broad aim of these stories, which is, quite simply, to honour God. Each one of them embodies a truth about living in this complex world, and they have been hard-learned lessons for me. You probably learned them a long time ago, but whether you did or you didn't I offer them with my love, and, above all, I do hope that you have a good read.

ADRIAN PLASS

# Nearly Cranfield

NANNA IS DEAD. Nanna is dead. Nanna is dead.

This so-called fact beat like a pulse in his brain all through the day and far into the night. They were only words, but they were frighteningly insistent, drumming and drumming and drumming away at the part of him that believed things, until he was almost too weary to resist. He'd known there was something wrong yesterday, on the Friday. Standing in the hall he'd overheard his mother talking in a low, troubled voice to his brother, Simon, on the stairs. He couldn't hear everything she said, but one whole phrase had floated clearly over the banisters: 'We all have to be very brave.'

He knew what that meant—something dark and horrible had happened. He didn't want to know what it was until his turn came round. There was a special order for being told about things in his family. After his mother and father had talked about whatever it was, it would be Betty's turn to hear next because she was twelve and the oldest child, then Simon, who was nine, and later, assuming that the subject was a suitable one for seven-year-old ears, he would be the last one to know.

He slept as well as ever on the Friday night. Nothing had even remotely happened until he actually knew about it, and he carefully banned guessing—indefinitely.

The air in the house was like thick grey porridge when he got up on Saturday morning. His mother had onion eyes and was too bright. Betty didn't tease him. Simon didn't speak. Dad looked as if he was trying to work out in his mind how to do some job he'd never done before. Dangerous, dangerous feelings rose up from inside him and stopped just before they got to the top. He made them stop. It was like putting off actually being sick till you got to the lavatory. He was good at that. They always said he was a good boy and better than Simon, because Simon just stood in the middle of the room and let it go all over the place and people did extra large sighs because they were sorry for him *and* they'd have to come back in a minute and clear it all up as well. Being sick was funny. He'd always thought it was really your stomach suddenly losing its temper with the last meal you had because it had said something rude, and ordering it out the way it came in with a loud roar. Sometimes. . . .

'Christopher, can we go upstairs for a moment? I want to have a little talk with you. Don't bother to put your things in the sink, darling, just come along with me.'

Upstairs—that meant it was a very big thing. You only went all the way upstairs for a little talk when it was a *very* big thing. Like when he'd done murals on the new wallpaper for Daddy, and Mummy wouldn't let Daddy talk to him till she had. But this wasn't going to be a telling off, he knew that. It was going to be something sad.

'Can I just go to the toilet first, Mum?' he said at the top of the stairs. 'I'll only be a moment.'

"Course you can, sweetheart. I'll be in our room.'

He turned the key carefully behind him in the lavatory door. There! He was locked in. If he stayed here for ever and didn't unlock the door again, he'd never hear about the sad thing and then it would never have happened. He sat on the edge of the lavatory and waited.

'Christopher, darling. Hurry up, there's a love.'

Mum was calling. He'd have to go. He stood irresolutely for a moment thinking that he'd been in the toilet too long to just do number one and not quite long enough to have done number two. He waited for a few more seconds then rattled the toilet-roll holder loudly and rustled the hanging length of pink tissue between the fingers and thumb of his right hand. Flushing the toilet had always been something he enjoyed. He would do it two or three times every visit if he was allowed. He just did it once now, then unlocked the door and turned to the left towards the bathroom, away from where his mother was waiting in the big bedroom.

'Just washing my hands, Mum,' he called.

'Good boy,' she responded automatically. 'Hurry up though.'

He washed his hands as well as he could. If he really had just done number two there would be trillions of germs rushing down the plughole now, choking and gasping on the microscopic mouthfuls of soap that were like poison to them. Remembering to turn the taps off, he gave the inside of the basin a perfunctory wipe and pulled the big yellow towel from the radiator. He dried each hand four times.

Four was his special number, and five was first reserve, but was hardly ever used because it got so sulky about having that spiky extra one hanging off at the corner. Four was nice. Settled and square. He loved four.

'My, oh my, nice and dry,' he chanted. That was what Nanna always said. . . .

Dropping the towel on the floor in a big yellow heap, he shot out of the bathroom and ran along the landing until he was just outside the big bedroom. Shoving his hands into his jeans pockets, he tried to feel ordinary and not unhappy, ready for when his mum had talked to him and it turned out to be nothing very much after all.

When he got into the bedroom his mother was sitting on the far side of the big bed with her back to him, looking out of the window. He stood by the door waggling one leg and hoping that she wouldn't pat the bed and ask him to come and sit beside her. That would be it if she did. That would really be it. He knew it would. Everything would go like a huge soft black quicksand, and he'd sink and sink until he cried.

'What, Mum?'

She laid a hand flat on the eiderdown beside her and smiled over her shoulder at him.

'Come and sit here, love. I want to tell you something.'

He jiggered over to her and plonked down on the bed, his hands still stuck in his pockets. He knew he'd got to sit there, but he didn't have to *be* there.

'Can I go an' buy a valve to blow up my football today, Mum? It's been soft for ages.'

With a little stab of helpless sympathy, he saw the hurt in his mother's eyes. She thought he cared more about a valve than about her needing him to be her little loving boy. No, Mum! No! I care, I care!

I'm here inside and I care!

'Sweetheart, there's something very sad I have to tell you. I've told the others and we're all being as brave as we can.'

Not Nanna. Not Nanna. Please, Mummy, don't tell me Nanna's dead. Don't tell me. . . .

'I'm afraid Nanna passed away in her sleep last night.'

Passed away? Did that mean she'd died?

'What's "passed away", Mum?'

His mother's eyes were all wet now, and she was shaking her head as if she'd run out of words. He'd done it all wrong. He'd known he was going to do it all wrong. She should have told him while he was standing by the door, then he could have worked up to being nice on his way over to her.

'Does it mean dead, Mum?'

She was crying properly now. She couldn't speak. She just nodded. Then Dad's voice came from the doorway.

'Pop off downstairs now, Chris. Mum's a bit upset. I'll be down in a minute.'

'Can I play with the Lego in my room, Dad?'

'Yes, good idea. Off you go.'

He listened outside the door for a moment. There was just murmuring at first, then he heard his mother's voice. It sounded hurt and puzzled.

'He didn't seem to react at all. Why didn't he cry or look upset? I don't understand it. He loved her so much.'

Back in his bedroom he pulled the big red plastic box from under his bed, and started to build a Lego house. He had loads and loads of Lego, given to him for birthdays and Christmas, or for no reason at all, which was usually best because it was a surprise. He decided to make a massive house that no one could break up, using every single tiny little piece of Lego in the box. He would put all the little Lego space-men and ambulance drivers and firemen and petrol-pump attendants onto the base, and build up the walls around them, then make a roof out of sloping blue pieces so that no one could get out at the top.

He thought about Nanna.

Nanna lived a very exciting half-hour bus journey away in Cranfield. From the top of the bus you could sometimes spot deer in the forest a while before you got to the first houses, and there was a fire station after that, which, if you were lucky, had its big doors open so that you could see the bright red engines inside like two huge toys. Then the bus stopped outside the baker's, but you didn't get off. You waited until you were nearly at the top of the hill that led out of the High Street, then you pressed the red button that rang the bell to tell the driver you wanted the request, and the bus stopped right at the top of the hill like a tired old monster, and you got off and you were there. You would feel as if you were crackling like a happy fire as you pulled your mum up the drive towards Nanna's green front door. Then a voice would call out through the letter-box, and it nearly always said the same thing.

'Who's this coming up my front path? Who's this coming to see me?'

Nanna was a bright light with grey hair and a green cardigan, and a spinning top that was old but still hummed, and a box full of wonderful things to make things with, and a drawer full of blown eggs, and a garden with pear trees, and lots of time to read stories, and stone hot-water bottles, and a Bible like a pirate's treasure-chest, and plans for being nice to people that you could help with, and she was the only other person in the whole world, apart from your mum and dad, who you'd take your clothes off in front of, and she was still there living in Cranfield right now, whatever anyone said, and tomorrow he would go there and see her and no one could stop him.

'All right, Chris?'

His dad was standing at the door looking worried.

'Yeah. . . . D'you like my house I've made, Dad? I'm going to Cranfield tomorrow.'

'I like it very much, Chris—it's really great. Better than I can do. There's no point in going to Cranfield, son. You heard what Mum said, didn't you?'

"Bout Nanna being dead, you mean?'

'Well . . . yes—you do know what that means, don't you?'

'Yep.'

'What do you think it means?'

'Like Sammy.'

His dad squatted down beside him, pleased.

'That's right, Chris, and you loved Sammy very much didn't you? Do you remember what we did when Sammy died?'

'Had a fureneral in the garden.'

'Funeral,' corrected his dad. 'That's right, and that's what'll happen with Nanna as well. Nanna's gone to be with Jesus, so she won't be needing her old body any more. Jesus will give her a new one. Do you understand?'

'Yes.'

'But that doesn't mean we don't feel sad about Nanna dying, does it? Because we loved her and we shall miss her very much.'

'Can we go to Cranfield tomorrow?'

He could tell his dad didn't want to get angry.

'Chris, have you listened to anything I've said? We're not going anywhere tomorrow, and we all have to be very kind and thoughtful to Mummy because she's very upset.'

There was a little pause. He wriggled inside. His dad spoke again.

'You're very upset about Nanna too, aren't you, Chris?'

'Mmmm. . . .'

He knew it wasn't enough. His dad wouldn't be able to help being a bit angry now. He was standing up and scratching his head and taking deep breaths.

'I just don't understand, Chris. I would have thought . . . well anyway, do your best to be a good boy and not make things difficult for everybody. Okay?'

'All right, Dad. I *am* going to Cranfield tomorrow, Dad.'

That was it.

'All right, Chris. You stay there and talk nonsense to yourself, but I've got too much to do to join in with you, I'm afraid. Just don't get in people's way!'

He'd let Dad make it all okay later on. It wasn't Dad's fault—he just didn't understand.

Saturday went on. Great aunts and rare aunts appeared. They moved heavily from room to room like big brown wardrobes on squeaky castors. He spent much of the day on the stairs. He was only allowed to sit on the even-numbered steps. If he sat on the odd ones he would be taken to a Japanese prisoner-of-war camp and tortured. The fourth one down was the safest. All the steps in Nanna's house were safe. The little squirrel in his stomach was very still whenever he went to Nanna's house. He was going there tomorrow. He was going to Cranfield tomorrow. He was going to see Nanna.

Nanna is dead.

Lying alone in the dark he fought those three words until long after the time when he usually went to sleep. Then, when he did slip into unconsciousness, he had one of the really bad dreams.

This time he was laying a big table for dinner. In his left hand was a basket containing knives, forks and pudding spoons. He was enjoying himself at first, walking slowly round the table putting a set of cutlery carefully at each place. He took a special pride in making sure that every knife and fork was absolutely straight, and that every dessert spoon pointed the same way. At last, his task complete, he took a step backwards to admire his handiwork. In the process, he happened to glance at the basket still hanging from his left hand. Then the horror began. There was a knife left in the basket. He had left one place without a knife. Terrible, nameless dread seized him as he rushed round the table at crazy, panic-stricken speed, desperately searching for the empty space so that he could put the mistake right before some hideous punishment was inflicted on him. Suddenly he saw the space, and with a little sob of joy, reached into the basket with his hand, only to find that the knife was gone. Then a door smashed open behind him and someone came in. . . .

No one went to church next morning. Dad did the breakfast. Betty took Mum's up on a tray. Simon went off out with a friend to play. The air was warm and quiet. A radio was on in the distance. Cars hummed round the corner by their house from time to time. A white dog tapped past on the smooth brick pavement at exactly nine fifty three. It tapped back again at one minute past ten. He watched everything from the window on the stairs and timed it on his watch with real hands. He'd asked specially for a watch with real hands. He hadn't wanted the other sort. Nanna had said, 'Digital, figital, fiddle-dee-dee!' He hadn't been able to say it. They'd laughed . . .

'I'm off now, Dad.'

Dad was looking at the paper, his eyes were dark

and tired. He looked up and frowned.

'Off? Off to where? What do you mean?'

'Cranfield. I'm going to Cranfield like I said, Dad.'

Dad leaned his head back on his chair and closed his eyes. He spoke in the weak, slow voice that meant he wasn't going to say anything else after he'd finished.

'Chris, you can go to Timbuctoo if you wish, for all I care just at the moment. If you want to go and play in the field, then for goodness' sake go! Make sure you're not late for lunch. Be careful. Goodbye.'

He could go to Timbuctoo if he wished. Timbuctoo was in Africa, in the Sahara desert. It was a lot further away than Cranfield. He decided to believe it was permission. He set off at ten-fifteen, with ten pence in his pocket and his very light blue anorak tied round his waist, to walk to Cranfield.

He knew the first bit very well because it was one of the walks they often did as a family. Turn right at the end of the village, walk straight across the common until he found himself on the black tarmac path, then follow the path until he came up to the very busy main road which had to be crossed if he wanted to get any further. If in doubt wait until you can't see or hear any traffic at all, then go straight over. He waited for a long time to make absolutely sure, then hurried across. Down the leafy track between the tall green trees, over the big flat car park where the fair came sometimes, down a little hill, and there he was at the place where he and Mummy caught the bus to Nanna's when Daddy didn't come. The next bit was easy too. Round the sharp corner by the sundial church and you were at the bottom of the long steep hill where you first started to get really excited about going to Nanna's. Cranfield was not till you got to the very top of this hill. It might even be a bit further than that. All you had to do was decide you were going to walk and walk and walk until you got there, and you had to *really* mean it, then it would happen.

He stopped at a little shop halfway up the hill to get some provisions for the rest of the journey. Sweets seemed a good idea because you could get enough with ten pence to make it look like a lot. He pulled one of the little white paper bags from the string where they hung, and filled it with the smallest cheapest sweets he could find, then took it to the lady at the counter and waited while she added it all up.

'Ten pence, dear, please.'

The lady was old and nice. He gave her his ten-pence piece.

'Bye then.'

'Bye.'

He felt good now that he had a full bag of sweets. Full things had a special, fat, rich feel. He decided that he wouldn't have a sweet until he'd walked another five hundred steps. By then he should be nearly at the top of the hill. If he wasn't, he would wait until he actually touched with his foot the first bit of pavement that was flat. That would make him carry on.

There was a cosy tingle in his stomach as he made these tough plans. He always enjoyed *really* meaning something.

Five hundred steps later, he wasn't even in sight of the top of the hill. He fixed his eyes on the ground and decided not to look up until he got there.

When he reached the top at last he stopped and lifted his head. The road swept down and away from him, curved up on the opposite side of the valley, and disappeared between fir trees in the far distance. No sign of Cranfield—not yet. It must be a lot further than he'd thought. Never mind. It was probably just past those trees on top of that other hill in front of him. He'd have one strawberry chew now, and nothing else until he got past those trees and could see what happened on the other side. All you had to do was walk and walk and walk until you got there.

It wasn't just past the trees, and it wasn't on the other side of the big roundabout, and it wasn't at the crossroads after the reservoir (though he did remember seeing that from the bus), and it wasn't at the end of a great long stretch of flat road between fields planted with something unbelievably, startlingly yellow, and it wasn't through a black, echoing railway arch, and it wasn't even just after the forest where, today, there were no deer.

He was running out of sweets. Just walk and walk.

Nanna bought him sweets sometimes.

'Let's put our coats on,' she'd say, 'and let's tiptoe down to the shops and buy ourselves a little treat.'

Sweets or a doughnut. She always let him choose. Then she'd do her real shopping. Shop to shop to shop they'd go, making each different place shine because they were in it being happy. Cranfield sparkled and shone like a Christmas tree because of Nanna. The butcher's shone. The butcher's meat shone. The post office twinkled. The kerb was made of precious grey stone. The houses glowed sweetly. The air had springs in it. Why should Jesus have Nanna all to himself?

He had one small gob-stopper left, and he was nearly there. He knew he was nearly there because he had come to the place where the bus turned right, away from the main road, and Mummy always said, 'Get your things together, Chris. We're nearly there.'

He turned to the right, took a few steps along the

quiet tree-lined avenue, then stopped and sat down on a low wall that bordered a graveyard beside a little dumpy grey church. Opposite him, right on the corner, was a signpost. It told him that Cranfield was only half a mile away. In a very short time he could be walking up Nanna's drive and waiting excitedly for the green door to open and the thin, familiar figure to put her arms out for one of their special cuddles.

The walk home was much worse than going. His legs were beginning to feel like jelly, and his stomach was rumbling and aching with hunger. The gob-stopper hadn't lasted very long, and it wasn't the sort of thing he wanted now anyway. As he trudged doggedly along the way he had come, he dreamed of thick jam sandwiches, meat and potatoes, apple pie and custard, sponge pudding with treacle poured over it, and big blocks of red and white ice-cream. It was Sunday, so they would've all had a jolly good dinner while he was away. Chicken probably. He wondered without much feeling whether Dad would smack him when he got back or just shout. Betty would be all big sister, and Simon would be extra nice and good, enjoying Chris being the naughty one. Mum would say, 'How could you, Christopher?' and let him off quite soon. He supposed he'd go to school tomorrow as usual. He didn't mind that. He liked school. Especially he liked his teacher, Miss Burrows. Her eyes lit up when he made a particular kind of joke, as though she'd peeped inside his head and knew what was going on in there. Nanna had been like that. Now that Nanna was dead, there was only Miss Burrows (and sometimes Dad when no one else was around) who really knew that funny bit of him.

Funny that he hadn't gone to Cranfield after all,

despite being so close. Sitting on that wall he'd suddenly felt cold and scared at the idea of seeing Nanna's house with its eyes shut and all the sparkle gone. He wouldn't have been able to lift the horse's head knocker and drop it again if he'd thought that the hollow, clonking noise had to travel through a sad, empty hall into a sad, empty kitchen where there was no one with flour over her hands who would drop whatever she was doing to come and let him in. He'd always wanted to be allowed to play with lots and lots of flour. He'd like to push his hands into its smooth crumbliness, and move them around underneath the surface, then walk around making white handprints on things and people. What would Mum and Dad say if he said he wanted a barrel of flour for his next birthday? Three guesses!

Just walk and walk and walk.

How long was it till his birthday? One—no, two months. That was about eight weeks, which was a long time until you suddenly got there and it was now. Dad had promised him a bike. He really, really hoped it wasn't going to be a good-as-new bike. He wanted a brand-new, shiny, perfect bike like the one Simon got last year, only better. There'd been talk of him having Simon's, but he didn't want Simon's. He wanted. . . .

He stumbled suddenly as a huge yawn seemed to take all the strength out of his body. He felt so tired now, but he hadn't got the energy to stop. All he could do was walk and walk like a walking robot until he came up against the longest brick wall in the world, or home or something. He noticed in a misty, dreamy sort of way that he was back at the edge of that busy main road that he'd crossed years and years ago this morning. Lots of cars and things roaring to and fro, but somehow he just didn't seem able to stop. . . .

'Chris! Christopher! Stop—don't move!'

He stood still, blinking at the frantically gesturing figure on the far side of the road. It was Dad. Dad had come to meet him. Good old Dad. Dad was coming over now. He was bending down and picking him up. It was very nice to be picked up, and Dad didn't seem angry at all. He seemed all soft and quiet and gentle, like someone who's had a big surprise that's made them feel shaky.

'Chrissy—Chris, where on earth have you been? I've been out looking for you for hours and hours. We've all been worried sick.'

The jogging motion of being carried was a very sleepy one.

'Been to nearly Cranfield, Dad. Told you I was, didn't I?'

'You told me? Chris, you never. . . .'

He could feel his dad remembering.

'You've walked to Cranfield and back, son?'

'Nearly, Dad. Can I have a jam sandwich when we get home, Dad?'

'Sixteen miles, Chris? We never thought . . . we told the police you'd gone to the field. Sixteen miles. . . .'

'Can I, Dad?'

'You can have the whole larder, Chrissy. Mum's still got your dinner on a plate for you. Why did you go?'

'Jus' wanted to—dunno.'

They were home. Dad knocked on the back door with his foot. Mum opened it and gave a little cry when she saw who it was. She held her arms out and suddenly he was being held by Mum instead of Dad. She wasn't angry either. She had a big smile on her face and tears were swimming around in her eyes. He'd never noticed how much Mummy looked like

Nanna before. She was Nanna's daughter, so it wasn't surprising really. Dad was standing close beside her still. They were both looking down at him.

'He's been to Cranfield,' said his dad softly.

'Mum?'

'Yes, my darling?'

'Nanna's dead, isn't she?'

'Yes, sweetheart, she is.'

Then he started to cry.

# A Letter to William

DEAR WILLIAM,

It was really marvellous to see you up at Euston the other day. The first time we've met in five years, and we only had seven minutes before my train went. I caught it by the skin of my teeth, incidentally. Into Bangor by three o'clock, and more or less straight onto the bus near the town clock after that. We arrived at Llanberis around four o'clock, and by quarter past I was sitting in the hotel cleaning my walking boots ready for the morning. Amazing really! I love trains—just as well really, the way things are with me at the moment. Actually, that's one of the main reasons for writing to you. I realized by the look on your face the other day that you were finding one or two of the things I said rather odd, to say the least. As far as I can remember, one chunk of our conversation went roughly as follows:

YOU: How come you're looking so fit?
ME: Well, it might have something to do with the fact that

I've climbed Snowdon seventy-odd times in the last six
 months.

YOU: *(After a convincing fish impression.)* You've what?

ME: I spend a lot of time climbing —

YOU: Yes, I heard what you said, but why on earth would
 you want to —

ME: *(Glancing at my watch and panicking.)* Look, I haven't time
 to explain now—it all started when I went to Scotland.

YOU: Scotland? Snowdon's in Wales, isn't it?

ME: Yes, of course it is, but—look, I'll write. Okay?

I haven't been able to forget that expression of
puzzled concern on your face as I flapped off with
my bags, so here I am, writing to put you out of your
misery. Only you'll have to bear with me. It's rather
a long story, and it starts more than nine months ago
when I was still teaching at that prep. school in
Bromley without any reason to believe that I'd ever
do anything else. Then something happened.

I had a phone call one evening from that chap
Dudley Nicholls. Think a bit and you'll remember
him. Same course as us at FE college. Fleshy fellow
with a deep voice and lots of money. Drove that big
estate car of his dad's as soon as he passed his test.
We used to cadge lifts off him quite a lot. He asked
us once if we thought you ought to take your socks
off when you make love in the back of a car, and you
said no, you didn't think that would be sufficient.
Derry Mimpson threw a cup of hot chocolate over
him when he was sitting in the next-door lavatory
once. He squealed and squealed, and you got cross
with Derry. Gottim? Good!

Now, do you also remember that about two-thirds
of the way through our second year, Dudley
changed suddenly and unaccountably? He started
smiling those funny crinkly smiles, and looking at us
as though we'd missed out on the treat of the
century. And he wouldn't come to the pub any

more, or smoke or swear, and he started sighing when one of us told a dirty joke, and in the end you told him that if he didn't tell us what was the matter with him you'd make him eat his car keys. So he told us. We were down behind the shrubbery at the end of the college gardens—remember? He went all glassy eyed and told us he'd become a Christian, and that he'd given his life to God, and given up all his bad ways, and was going to lots of Bible studies and prayer meetings and goodness knows what else at this little church he'd found behind the wool shop in Station Road. I was all ready to take the micky, but you were really nice to him, William, you really were. I can see you now, nodding seriously and saying what a good thing it was to find something to really believe in.

Then he said would we come to one of the services, and you said you knew about that sort of church and that, although you respected people who went, there were too many meetings and too much about what you shouldn't do and not enough about actually *doing* things, and I just sort of agreed with you, so we didn't go. We didn't see so much of him after that, did we?

Anyway, he and I kept in touch after we all left college, and later he became an assistant manager in a supermarket down near Sevenoaks, so we weren't really living that far apart. I knew he still went to church, although he didn't talk about it all that much. We used to meet for lunch once a month or so. He liked talking about the old college days mostly. Got quite wistful. Used to mention you a fair bit, William. I think he respected you a lot (can't think why!).

Where was I? Ah, yes—the phone call. He sounded a bit odd on the phone—puzzled and strained perhaps. He said he wanted to talk to me, ask me about something, and could he come up that Saturday on the train and spend a couple of hours at my place. I was quite intrigued, and I told him to come by all means. Told him I'd meet him at the station and all that, and asked him if he could give me some idea of what it was all about. There was silence at the other end of the line for a while, then he spoke.

'I've found an ad in the paper—well, not an ad, a sort of announcement, and I don't know what to do about it. I want to know what you think.'

That's what he said, and that was all he'd say about it on the phone, so we said goodbye and that was that until Saturday. I don't mind telling you, William, I was a trifle nervous about me in the role of advice-giver. To be honest, I think old Dudley saw me in a sort of 'Williamish' aura. If you'd been around, you're the one he'd have gone for. Still— you weren't, and he couldn't.

So, there we were on the Saturday, Dudley and I sitting opposite each other in my sitting-room. We'd gone past the 'How are you? Would you like a cup of coffee?' stage, and Dudley took this folded sheet of newspaper from his inside pocket and passed it across. I spent a couple of very bewildering minutes studying a recipe for home-made marmalade before Dudley realized I was looking at the wrong side and made me turn it over. On the other side was this ad-cum-announcement—must have been about quarter-page size—and it was, as Sherlock Holmes might have put it, very singular. I'll write it out for you now, as near as I can remember it, just as it appeared on the page:

UNITED KINGDOM CHRISTIAN RECRUITMENT CENTRE
HALSTER, SCOTLAND.
WE ARE NOW THE SOLE AGENTS FOR SALVATION ET AL

IN ENGLAND, WALES, SCOTLAND AND NORTHERN
IRELAND.
VISITORS WARMLY WELCOMED.
NO APPOINTMENTS NECESSARY.
CAUTION: PREVIOUS ARRANGEMENTS MAY <u>NOT</u> BE
VALID.
WE WILL ADVISE WITH PLEASURE.

As you can see, there's no telephone number, and as for the address—well, whoever's heard of Halster? Now, you're going to smile when you read this next bit, and I don't blame you. It sounds ridiculous, but it's true. There was a sort of glow all around that bit of the page. I'm not kidding, there really was. I remember blinking and shaking my head to get rid of it, but it wouldn't go. It was in the page, or in the air around the page, or—something. When I looked up Dudley was nodding and smiling in an excited sort of way.

'You can see it too, can't you?' he said.

'The shininess, you mean?'

'Yes,' he said, and he leaned over, took the paper from my hand, and smoothed it out flat on the coffee table between us. 'Not everyone sees it, you know—most people don't. The thing is. . . .'

You remember what a worrier Dudley used to be. We used to say he looked just like Tony Hancock when there was something on his mind. Well, he looked just like that now, except that there was this excitement queueing up to appear on his face as well.

'The thing is,' he went on, 'that I don't know whether being able to see it means you're . . . well, all right, or whether it means . . . something else.'

How I wished you were there, William. I was completely flummoxed. Shiny newspapers? Sole agents for salvation? I seemed to hear the gates of the funny farm clanging shut behind me as Dudley's deep voice motored on.

'I'm going up there. I'm going to go up to Halster to find this place and ask them if I'm really . . . well, ask them for some advice on . . . things.'

Well, you know me, William. It costs nothing to humour someone, and nobody ever really wants advice if it doesn't agree with what they're going to do anyway, so I just nodded and shrugged a bit and said, 'Why not?' and things like that. Dudley stared down at the paper for a minute when I'd finished, and when he looked up he was biting one side of his lower lip and looking a little uneasy.

'The thing is, Ray,' he said through his chewed lip, 'I don't fancy going all the way up there on my own, so I was going to ask if you'd come with me.'

Guess who suddenly got very objective. 'What about the cost?' I asked him. 'I'm broke.'

'I'll pay,' said Dudley.

A free trip to Scotland. My objectivity took a bit of a nose dive, but I felt I ought to keep trotting out the arguments against—for Dudley's sake.

'I can't just up and leave the school,' I pointed out. 'It's my job. I won't get time off during the term.'

Dudley nodded—he'd thought of that. 'It's only a fortnight or so until the Easter holidays,' he said, 'and I can get a week off then, no problem. What do you say? Go on, say you'll come.'

Well, the only objection left was the obvious one, wasn't it?

'Look, Dudley,' I said, as gently as I could, 'I'm sure I'd enjoy a trip up to Scotland very much, and it's very generous of you to offer to stand the expenses, but have you thought about how you're going to feel when you get up to this God-fors. . . this place, and find that there is no Christian recruitment centre or whatever they call themselves?'

'I don't mind taking the risk,' Dudley replied

earnestly, 'and anyway, what about the glow—the shininess? You can't explain that away, can you?'

I picked up the piece of paper again and peered closely at it. The glow was still there, a faint, whitish light that seemed quite separate from the substance of the paper itself. I turned it over and stared at the marmalade recipe again. No glow there, nothing at all. I held the sheet up flat and level with my eyes, the announcement uppermost, but out of my vision. To my surprise there was no sign of the mysterious light rising above the surface of the paper. Very strange indeed.

'Tell you what, Dudley,' I said at last, 'you let me take this paper to a friend of mine who's a chemist, and if he says it's just ordinary paper with nothing in it to account for the light effect, then I'll come with you. Agreed?'

'Agreed!' said Dudley.

So off I went after school on the Monday to a chap called David Stolle (you wouldn't know him) who runs the chemistry department at one of the polys in town. Too harassed to breathe as usual, he passed me on to one of his research assistants who promised to do the business and post the results—and the paper—back to me before the end of the week. I suppose I was quite excited when the envelope arrived on Friday. I know I tore it open as soon as it plopped onto the mat that morning. Couldn't make sense of it at first, William. You know how thick I can be with printed stuff. Eventually, though, I gathered that the list of compounds that the chemist fellow had typed out were all perfectly normal ones, and as for anything that could produce the kind of glowing effect I'd described—well, there was nothing. Not only that, but the fellow had added in a rather terse note at the bottom that he hadn't been able to see any kind of glow on the paper anyway, so perhaps I had been mistaken in my original observations. Bit shirty I guessed.

Then, rather gingerly, I took the folded piece of newspaper out of the envelope and opened it up slowly and carefully. Had I been dreaming last Saturday? No, I hadn't. You'll just have to take my word for it, William. That announcement shone just like it had before, and I had to accept that there was no way of explaining it. Later that day I rang Dudley and told him the trip was on.

Believe it or not, William, but as the days went by I began to get quite excited about our safari into deepest Scotland. And when I say *deepest* Scotland, that's exactly what I mean. I found a big map of Scotland at school and brought it home with me. Imagine how I felt on discovering that Halster was a tiny village way up on the west coast, just about as far away as anywhere could be without crossing the sea to some remote island.

'How come,' I said to Dudley on the phone that evening, 'the *sole* agents for salvation are tucked away in the back of beyond where no one can get at them?'

'How come,' replied Dudley with unaccustomed alacrity (good phrase that, eh, William?), 'that Jesus was born in a stable?'

I gave him that one.

School finished on Friday. Dudley came up after work that evening and stayed the night so that we could set off sharp in the morning. I woke up at some absurd hour and had an 'I must be a loony' attack. But it passed, and by the time we were out on the road the next day, enjoying one of those deliciously crisp early spring mornings, I was just glad to be going somewhere. You know how it is when you set out on these really long journeys. Mild ecstasy for the first hour, then a period of quiet horror when you realize just how far you've still got to go, and then you sort of settle down and sleep or chat or listen to the radio and accept that you'll probably never do anything but sit in a car for the rest of your life. Mind you, I couldn't complain about lack of comfort. Dudley had one of those great big foreign cars that pumps itself up before starting. Huge inside. Not bad on an assistant super-market manager's salary, eh? Something told me Mum and Dad were still footing one or two of their little Dudley's bills, not that I said anything, of course. Good for him, I thought.

We did pretty well that first day, ending up in some town a little to the south of Carlisle. We spent the night in a grotty little hotel beside a main road. Poor old Dudley was so bushed by then that we'd decided to stop at the next place we came to, and 'The Lay-By' was it. (I still don't drive by the way, and, no, I still don't know why not, William. Okay?) Dudley had something to eat and then dragged himself off to bed, and I decided to watch a bit of television in the 'Lounge'. The 'Lounge' turned out to be a large cupboard full of armchairs with a portable, black-and-white television on a shelf in the corner. The only other occupant of the room was a large elderly lady who introduced herself as Mrs Jones. She said she'd been staying at 'The Lay-By' for some years, and thought she'd probably die there because she had no family left and didn't get about much now because her hip was so bad. She was a nice old thing. I ended up telling her about our trip, and what started it off, and she said could she see the advert. Well, I hadn't actually mentioned the 'glow', but after she'd unfolded the sheet of paper, found her glasses in her bag, and peered at the printed words for a minute or so, she said, 'Ooh! Look at that! It's all shiny!' So then we talked about that, and I told her about Dave Stolle's report—his assistant's report I mean—and she made me copy the words from the announcement onto a page in a tiny little notebook that she fished out of her bag. And when she looked at the words I'd written, she said, 'It shines in my little book too.' Blow me down if she wasn't absolutely right! There was a sort of scaled-down glow on that little sheet of paper, just like on the big one. I shivered all the way down my back when I saw that. Anyway, I went off to bed soon after that. Mrs Jones wasn't up by the time we left early in the morning, but I mention that little chat I had with her for a special reason which I'll tell you about later.

I can't remember if you've ever been to Scotland, William. I hadn't. It's just plain breathtaking. By the time we'd passed Loch Lomond and driven between these two mountains standing like giant gate-posts at the south end of Glen Coe, I felt just about gorged with beautiful scenery. Then there was a car ferry to get across to the peninsular where Halster was situated, and last of all we had to take a long, narrow, winding road through countryside that was all heather and cragginess, until we quite suddenly found ourselves in a little sloping village that, by our calculations, had to be Halster. It really was small, William. A single street lined with little dark grey cottages— sorry—crofts, and down at the far end, a wedge-shaped deep blue area. That was the sea. There were two shops, one of them more of a trading post than anything else, and a church, grey like the crofts, but bigger. Then there was one pub with a sign saying that bed and breakfast was available, and that was about it really.

We parked the car in a space next to the church and walked slowly along the street feeling a bit down. We'd come an awful long way and I suppose

I'd expected somehow that this place, this recruitment centre, would be a golden palace-like building, impossible to miss. It was a bit of an anticlimax to actually be in Halster and find only the two rows of crofts, mostly single storey, with their tiny weatherproof windows and low front doors. We decided to try one of the shops. Shopkeepers knew most things, we reckoned. We were right. A long, thin, very Scottish gentleman in the little general store was as helpful as we could have wished. Obviously, we were by no means the first travellers to ask about our particular destination.

Back to the car we went, quite enlivened again now, and a couple of minutes later we turned up a narrow, north-pointing dirt track near the top end of the village. Ten minutes later we were there. It still wasn't very impressive, but at least we knew we were in the right place. On a tattered wooden notice-board set at the entrance to what looked like a farmyard were the words 'Christian Recruitment Centre' painted in big yellow letters. We left the car next to a big Land-Rover-type vehicle beside one of the outhouses and walked across to the biggest building, the farmhouse we supposed, and knocked on the door. It was late afternoon by then, William. There was a viciously cold wind blowing through that farmyard, and the countryside around was just a dark frowning mass. For two pins I'd have run for the car at that moment and cleared off back to anywhere where there was lots of noise and light and ordinariness. Then the door opened.

When I say that the door was opened by an elderly man with lots of white hair and what I always think of as a sailor's beard and twinkling eyes and a pipe clenched between his teeth, and that suddenly I didn't want to clear off after all, that doesn't really tell you a hundredth of what I thought and felt.

When I was a kid, I used to have a particular dream sometimes. In this dream I'd arrived at the place where I needed to be. Don't ask me where it was. It was just—right. There was lovely music and this soft weepy feeling in my stomach. My parents were there and we were all smiling. I think there were coloured lights too, and a sort of deep bubbling excitement about what was going to happen next. Someone was coming, I think.

Anyway, that was a bit how I felt when the door opened and this genial old character ushered us into what was clearly the farmhouse kitchen, and sat us down at the big old table in the centre of the room. I felt so warm and light and—sorry, I'm rabbiting on again. I'll get on with it. When we were all settled with a mug of hot cocoa—delicious stuff—our host leaned back in his chair and smiled at us through his pipe smoke.

'Right,' he said in his rumbly voice, 'my name's Angerage—Bill Angerage. Who are you two fine chaps?'

We introduced ourselves.

'And what can I do for you?' he asked.

'I want to be a Christian,' blurted out old Dudley, 'or rather I. . . .'

He didn't get any further. Our new friend's face lit up like a beacon. He jumped to his feet, came round the table, and smacked Dudley heartily on the back as though he'd just heard the most wonderful news in the world.

'Marvellous! Marvellous!' he kept saying. 'That's really marvellous! You've really made my day, young man!'

He would have hugged Dudley if he could I think, but the 'young' man who'd made his day was curled back in his chair, a bit overwhelmed. Very pleased though, I could tell. Then he turned to me, his eyes all alight and hopeful.

'You too, Ray? Do you want to join us as well?'

I was very confused inside, William. That's why my answer was so pathetic.

'I only came along to keep Dudley company,' I said, my voice all high-pitched and strangled.

'Ah, well,' said Bill, staring at me for a moment, 'you're here, you're here. Now, down to business.'

He went back and sat down again on the other side of the table.

'Now, as you'll have realized from our little ad in the paper, things have changed a lot—radically I might say. The whole business of prayer, Bible study, church services, et cetera, has been scrapped. Direct order from HQ. All that sort of stuff goes out the window. No need any more for discussions about salvation by faith, or about who's in and who's out. The whole thing's been completely redesigned. You can still get total forgiveness, eternal life, love, joy and peace, the whole package as before, but the terms are different—very different.'

Dudley's brow was furrowed with puzzlement and worry.

'But, Mr Angerage. . . .'

'Call me Bill, Dudley, there's a good chap.'

'Bill, er . . . all those things you said don't matter any more. If we don't have those—I mean, what's left? What do we have to do?'

'Aah!' said Bill richly, pulling on his briar with deep relish. 'Now we come to it. What indeed?' He chuckled to himself for a moment, then folded his arms on the table and leaned towards Dudley, his pipe jutting out at an angle from the side of his mouth. 'All you have to do, my friend, is climb Snowdon three times every week.'

Some silences are very loud, aren't they? This one was. Eventually, all the things that had rushed around in the quietness flowed down and were condensed into the single tiny word that Dudley said after a long pause.

'Why?'

Bill raised a hand so that he could wag his finger.

'Ours not to reason why, mate. If HQ says that's the way it's to be done, then that's the way it's to be done. Faith—that's what you need. The instructions are very simple. Snowdon—three times a week.'

'And there's no other way to get forgiveness and—all the rest?'

Bill shook his head. 'No other way, my friend,' he said slowly. 'Worth it though, isn't it?' he queried, his eyes twinkling even more than before.

'Oh, yes—yes, of course,' answered Dudley, but I could see his mind was working hard on this new idea.

'But what happens about my job, Bill? I mean, I wouldn't be able to carry on with what I'm doing now, would I? Good heavens. . .' Dudley's eyes opened wide as the implications of the thing became clearer. 'It must take a day to climb right up Snowdon and back again, so that means three days plus travelling. I'd hardly have time to do anything, let alone get a decent job of any kind. I wouldn't have any money. I wouldn't. . . .'

'What about your parents, Dudley?' I interrupted. 'Isn't there a chance that they'd. . . .'

Dudley flushed. 'No,' he said dismally. 'They'll give me just about anything I want if I go on living nearby, but they've made it clear ever since I left college that if I ever move right away from them, then that's it. I'm on my own. I don't think whizzing home from Wales for flying visits a couple of times a week would count as living nearby. Besides,' he added rather pathetically, 'I don't really like travelling all that much.'

'Don't you think,' said Bill gently, 'that the travelling or even living in Wales itself, might be worth it if you get eternal life and happiness in return? After all, you travelled all the way up here, didn't you? That's our first screening process after you're attracted by the light. Well, here you are. You've got this far.'

Dudley was tracing the shape of a stain on the table top with his finger. He spoke without looking up.

'Do some people come all the way up here and then decide not to . . . go ahead then?'

'The vast majority,' said Bill, his eyes sad for the first time since we'd met him. 'Some try to compromise despite the fact that I always make it quite clear that the three climbs are an absolute base-line minimum.'

'How do they compromise then?'

'Well, there's one church down in the South for instance. The minister came up here—he'd seen the ad just like you—said he agreed with everything I said, went off happily back home and wrote me a letter a few weeks later to say that he'd discussed the whole thing with the church council and they'd come up with an 'inspired idea'. They hired a carpenter to construct a four-foot-high model of Snowdon with two steps going up one side and two going down the other. Every Sunday, each member of the congregation has to go up one side and down the other. They've built it into the service. It comes just between the third hymn and the sermon.'

'And that doesn't count?' said Dudley, obviously hoping that it might.

'It's not climbing Snowdon three times a week,' said Bill.

Silence reigned for another minute or two. Dudley took a biro and a piece of paper from his inside pocket and started to write something. His brow was puckered and there were many crossings out. Bill just sat puffing his pipe and watching patiently. At last, Dudley looked up.

'Bill, listen!' he said earnestly. 'I've just been thinking. There must be other jobs that need doing, besides the actual climbing. Supposing I adapted all the choruses we sing in our church at the moment so that they fitted the new way of things?' Another and even greater inspiration seized him. 'We could call it *The Snowdon Songbook.*'

Bill was slowly shaking his head, but Dudley seemed quite carried away by the idea.

'Look, I've just been trying one or two out. Er . . . this one for instance: "Hallelujah, I'm a Christian." You know the one I mean. This is what it sounds like when its changed. Listen—listen!'

Dudley held his piece of paper in one hand and began to sing the words he had written in a feverishly joyful voice:

> 'Hallelujah, I'm a climber,
> I climb all day,
> I climb up Snowdon,
> Climb all the way.
> Hallelujah, I'm a climber,
> I climb all day.'

I looked away in embarrassment. Bill started to speak. 'Dudley, I don't think. . . .'

But there was no stopping old Dudley.

'Just a minute, just a minute!' he said. 'What d'you think about this one? Used to be "Marching to Zion". Listen!'

The awful voice started once more in some strange alien key:

> 'We're marching to Snowdon.
> Beautiful, beautiful Snowdon,

> We're marching upward to Snowdon,
> The beautiful mountain of God.

'And what about this one:

> What a friend we have in Snowdon,
> All our—'

'No, Dudley!' Bill's voice was no louder than before, but it contained a note of authority now that cut Dudley off in mid-warble. 'It's no good simply singing about it. You've got to do it. You've got to climb Snowdon three times every week.'

He swung a hand out in the vague direction of the rest of Scotland.

'Why, I could take you to a place only a few miles from here where they've set up Snowdon counselling services, Snowdon discussion groups, and courses in 'The real meaning of climbing'. But none of them actually do it. One of our chaps who comes from that same town, and pops up from Wales very occasionally, isn't allowed into any of those groups because he's 'in error' with his simplistic approach to Snowdon. No, Dudley, if you want to write some songs to keep you going while you're on the slopes, then that's fine—good idea in fact! But not instead of. Won't wash with HQ, you see.'

Dudley was really chewing at that old lip now, William. And his eyeballs were dancing about all over the place as he tried to think of a way to get what he wanted and keep what he'd got.

'What about friends?' he said feebly. 'How do I keep up with all my friends? I'll never see them. They'll think I'm mad. They'll think. . . .'

Dudley's voice trailed away. You could see he was answering his own questions in his head. Hadn't quite given up yet, though. He banged the table with the flat of his hand suddenly and sat bolt upright.

Obviously thought he'd hit on a winner.

'I'm not fit! I won't get up there—not even once. It's not fair! What about that?'

Bill nodded patiently. He'd heard it all before, I expect.

'You turn up and climb as far as you can, and we'll make sure you get to the top from there, even if you have to be carried to the nearest mountain railway stop. Don't worry! Young chap like you, you'll be fit as a fiddle in no time. Wouldn't surprise me if you were nearly running up inside a fortnight.'

Well, that was about it really, William. Dudley didn't have anything else to say, and this Bill Angerage didn't say much more either. He told Dudley to go home and think about it, and if he decided to go ahead to drop him a line and he'd fix it all up and arrange some help with the practical side of things. He looked at me when he said that as well.

I've never known anything as cold and dark as that farmyard after Bill closed the front door of the house behind us. We stayed at the pub that night in Halster, and started driving back the next morning, talking all the way about the things we wished we'd asked but didn't.

As soon as I got home, I sat down and wrote two letters. One was to the headmaster of my school, giving a term's notice. The other was to Bill Angerage at the Christian Recruitment Centre, saying that I wanted to do the Snowdon thing. And that, William, together with bits of part-time work, is what I've been doing for the last six months or so. It's very tough, but I have got very fit. And there are other things . . . but I'll tell you about them when we meet again. Do me a favour will you, William. Find the bit where I copied out the advert for you and have another look at it. If you can see a sort of

44

shininess around it, well ... give it some thought anyway.

Dudley? Well, he's still chewing it all over, and I'm still working on him when I can. I think he'll make the right decision in the end.

Oh, and Mrs Jones—the old lady in the hotel, remember? I met her down in Llanberis a couple of weeks ago. She was in a wheelchair, and just about to do the two or three yards she can manage at the foot of the first slope, before going down to get the train. She was in terrific spirits. Said she'd never been so happy in her life. Great, eh?

One more thing, William. I said Dudley didn't say anything else to Bill Angerage after his 'I'm not fit enough' speech, but there was one thing. It was when we got to the door. Dudley stopped in the doorway and, as far as I can remember, this is what he said:

'I don't see what was so wrong with the old way anyway. The people in my church never did anyone any harm. Why do you want to go and make it all so much harder?'

'You really don't understand, do you?' said Bill. 'We haven't made it harder, we've made it much easier.'

See you on the slopes one day?

    Yours,

    Ray.

# Why It Was All Right To Kill Uncle Reginald

My Solicitor, Miss Cudlip, has requested that I provide a detailed account of my reasons for executing Uncle Reginald and a full description of the means by which I accomplished the task. This I am more than pleased to do. I would, however, like to make two points first, both of which are crucial to an accurate understanding of my position.

(a) I am *not* in favour of murder or any other crime. I have, throughout my life, been an exemplary citizen. In forty years I cannot, immodest though the claim must seem, recall a single instance of deliberate illegality. Furthermore, my morality with regard to 'relationships' has been consistently sound. As far as I can tell I have caused emotional hurt to no person, nor have I succumbed to the lure of brief amorous adventures as many men seem to. Miss 'Right' may possibly appear at some point, but if she does not then I am content.

As to my work, I have been employed for the last

twenty years as chief assistant (there is one young person underneath me) at a shop which retails smart, traditional clothing, and I should be most surprised if Mr Robards, the manager, were to offer any but positive comments on my behalf.

My original decision to accommodate Uncle Reginald over the last ten years was, furthermore, based on charitable motives. One of my poor mother's final requests was that, when she died, and her room became available, I should invite her brother Reginald to live with me in the house that I would, of course, inherit from her. Mother did not actually frame this as a request, more perhaps in the form of an instruction. After her death I was naturally no longer obliged to carry out her wishes, but a certain mental discomfort prompted me, voluntarily, to remember her words as a plea rather than an order. Accordingly, I invited Uncle Reginald to sell his large house in Eastbourne and move into my much humbler little dwelling near Heathfield. A retired insurance person, relatively fit and of exceedingly regular habits, he seemed an ideal person with whom to share my home, and I experienced none but familial and benevolent feelings towards him for the whole of the first year that he was in situ.

My first point in brief, then, is that I am not the murdering type of person and that what has happened *cannot* be classified as murder. Like killing in wartime and the destruction of dangerous wild creatures, my execution of Uncle Reginald was wholly justified and I am quite certain that there is not a judge and jury in the land who, having examined the evidence, would not be anxious to speedily expedite my return to my own little home and the good offices of Mr Robards, who must be severely stretched with a solitary young person on his staff. But what, you may ask, is this evidence of which I speak? This leads me into my second point.

(b) In the bottom drawer of the walnut bureau in the hall at the foot of the stairs, you will find two cardboard containers, each measuring approximately six inches by three inches. Each one is labelled on one of the large sides in thick orange marker-pen. The top one is entitled *Breakfast,* and the bottom one *Lunch,* or it may possibly be *Sunday Lunch.* Each box contains a video tape of Uncle Reginald consuming a meal, and it is essential that this statement should be read in conjunction with the screening of these visual documents. I imagine that it is entirely possible for a large-screened television set to be made available in the courtroom for the benefit of jurors. I would myself not be at all averse to reading this account from the witness-box, while all others present view my two little programmes in the order that I have already listed them. I have no doubt whatsoever that all who see Uncle Reginald in action at the table will not only applaud my subsequent decision, but will heartily wish that they themselves had been permitted to be partakers in his dissolution.

The substance of my second point, then, is that there is more than ample evidence of my complete sanity, the video tapes and this document being the bulk of that evidence. In addition there is my own general demeanour. I make it a point never to express anger or resentment to others, despite (as you shall shortly hear) extreme provocation from Uncle Reginald. I recall, for instance, an occasion when Mr Robards felt it necessary to be quite scathingly critical about a window-display over which I had worked for many hours. Despite the intensity of my inner feelings I merely nodded patiently and agreed to alter completely what I considered to be a most pleasing arrangement. Not only that, but when, later that same day, Mr Robards, in the course of negotiating the very narrow and poorly lit stairs down to our little staff lavatory, tripped over a box that I had inadvertently left on the second step and fell heavily onto the concrete floor below suffering quite severe bruising, I displayed not a trace of pleasure or satisfaction. On the contrary I helped him to his feet, bade him sit quietly in the easy chair at the rear of the shop, and prepared a mug of hot, sweet tea to restore his nerves. Does an insane person exhibit such self-control? I think not.

If any further indication of my healthy mental state is required, there is the manner in which I set about the preparation of my televisual record of Uncle Reginald's abominable practices. I made the decision to enquire into the possibilities of video tape recording, only after it had become clear that execution was the only appropriate response to the unspeakable things that I was forced to witness and endure day after day.

It seems strange (to digress a little) that a whole year passed before the range and repulsiveness of my Uncle's eating habits began to impress them-selves upon me. Certainly I had perceived a remark-able consistency of pattern in his behaviour at the table, but our general relations had been good, if quiet, and I tended to regard his predictability as a virtue rather than a vice. I believe that the first thing to jar unpleasantly upon me was the click in Uncle Reginald's jaw. When I say in his jaw I mean, of course, that it was a click that occurred when Uncle Reginald was using his jaws, when he was chewing in other words. Let me say immediately that it was not a loud click, nor did it occur with every masticatory movement of the jaw. It was the sound one might make by flicking a thumbnail against a fingernail on the same hand, and for some physiological reason that is beyond my comprehension, it seemed to occur on every alternate closing motion of the mouth. When I add that each click was accompanied or instantly followed by an infinitesimal but unmistakable lateral movement of the upper jaw as it met the lower, you will perhaps begin to sense the horror of my position. I do not wish to embarrass the Court with gratuitous obscenities, but I think it important to my case to point out that, occasionally, a fragment of non-solid food would be resting on the lower lip at the moment when the upper lip descended. The effect of the lateral jaw movement in this case was to smear the food along the lower lip and on occasions to spurt a tiny amount of it onto the outer edge of that same lower lip or even, but much more rarely, onto his chin, which was covered with wiry red whiskers.

Naturally, the observation and identification of these details and patterns took place over a period of many months, but certainly, by the time Uncle Reginald had been living in my house for eighteen months, I was occupied for the majority of each meal-time that we spent together, with the nightmare of awaiting each individual click and each tiny untoward movement of the jaw. My own eating I developed into a virtually soundless activity so that I should miss no detail of the foul performance before me. I was particularly clever in the way in which I learned to impale and cut food without my knife or fork coming into contact with the plate, thus avoiding those loathsome scraping and clacking noises which notoriously result from the contact of steel on china. Once I had mastered this skill to the point where I could consume meals not only soundlessly but with the barest and most infrequent glances at my own plate, I was able to give my full attention to Uncle Reginald's nauseous activities which, over the next few months, I discovered to my horror, were far from being confined to the details I had already noticed. To my amazement I discovered that every single aspect of my Uncle's ingestive behaviour possessed the same repulsive quality. After more than eight years of studying, listing and inwardly digesting the full facts of the case, I knew that Uncle Reginald should be executed and that I was to be the agent.

I procured my video equipment from a small but reputable firm whose retail outlet is situated in a long, busy road of shops which runs parallel to the promenade in the seaside town that lies a few miles to the south of Heathfield. I was advised and assisted by a most amiable and helpful young man who, very early on in the proceedings, made the false but quite understandable assumption that I required equipment for the purpose of recording the activities of domestic pets of some kind. It seemed wise to allow this misunderstanding to continue, as the technical problems and demands appeared to be similar, especially with regard to the matter of recording small and not easily distinguishable sounds, such as hamsters squeaking (or jaws clicking). I learned that my best plan would be to arrange what I believe the young man referred to as an 'add on' microphone at a point as close as possible to the sound source in question. As to the all-in-one camera and recording machine, a model was available which combined two very desirable virtues. It was extremely easy for a novice to operate and very little in the way of extra lighting was needed over and above the level of light one might find in an average kitchen lit by the type of strip lighting that is installed in my own house. My adviser suggested that a small spotlight of the domestic variety would be an ideal adjunct to the normal illumination of the room, and as I already possessed such an appliance, the business of lighting required no further consideration.

In the matter of payment, I received an extremely welcome surprise. Expecting that it would be necessary to purchase the equipment, I had taken my building society book from the top drawer of the bureau and was quite prepared to draw out whatever sum was needed for the purpose. (My account had swollen at the time of Mother's death, and much interest had accrued since then.) Imagine my pleasure on learning that is was possible to hire the camera and microphone for a total of thirty pounds for an entire weekend. I left the shop with my equipment, a book of operating instructions, and a deep sense of well-being at the accomplishment of the first part of my plan.

That evening, after Uncle Reginald had retired to bed at nine forty-seven as usual, I set up the camera in a corner of the kitchen and focused on the back of Uncle Reginald's chair. I then connected one end of the microphone lead to the camera recorder, and having laid the kitchen table for breakfast, placed the microphone itself on a small plastic stand (supplied by the shop) so that it was pointing towards a spot midway between Uncle Reginald's cereal bowl and the place where his face would normally be during the act of consumption. When I was satisfied that all was as it should be, I went up to my own bedroom but was unable to sleep for some time owing to an excess of excitement and anticipation concerning the following day. Despite this, however, I am totally sure that if someone had quite suddenly switched on my bedroom light as I lay on my back in bed, they could have detected not so much as a flicker on my face or in my posture to betray that excitement. I believe my fists may have been slightly clenched, but that was all.

In the morning (Saturday morning) I arose early and unclamping the small spotlight from the second bookshelf down beside my window, I carried it downstairs, and after attaching it to one side of the small cupboard in the top of the kitchen cabinet, adjusted the angle of its beam until it covered the area soon to be occupied by the top half of Uncle Reginald's body. My sole remaining task before all preparations were complete was to account to Uncle Reginald for the sudden appearance of the appliance facing him from the corner of the room and the microphone standing beside his place on the table. This was rendered quite simple by two things: my uncle's vague geniality (in matters other than eating) and the existence of Cousin Hubert in New Zealand. Hubert is the only child of my mother's older brother Desmond (now deceased). He writes very infrequently and has had no actual contact with relatives at home for thirty years. I informed Uncle Reginald that Hubert had written to me requesting photographs of surviving members of the family, and in particular his Uncle Reginald, of whom he retained very fond memories despite the long period since their last meeting. I had decided, I said, to send Hubert a video tape rather than photographs, and over the weekend I would be recording brief extracts from an appropriately commonplace activity—namely the eating of meals—so that Hubert would be able to witness our ordinary, family, day-to-day living. I added that the equipment would sometimes be operating and sometimes not, thus implying that I had some kind of remote control over the machinery, and that

Uncle Reginald should do nothing out of the ordinary for the benefit of the camera. I also pointed out that I would, from time to time, need to leave the table to refocus or adjust the lens, and apologized in advance for the disruption this would cause in our customarily well ordered meal-times.

Uncle Reginald's response to my remarks was precisely as I had anticipated. He appeared pleased, if a little surprised, that Hubert held him in such fond regard, and he was impressed but totally baffled by my television equipment. By the end of Saturday he had become quite accustomed to my occasional departures from the table to make adjustments to the camera, and the constant presence of the microphone no longer seemed to register in his consciousness. The whole day was a perfect rehearsal for Sunday, the day on which I planned to actually imprint Uncle Reginald's crimes onto video tape. That night, lying in my bed, my self-control was severely stretched. It was as though a series of small but thrilling electric shocks were being administered to various parts of my body. How I remained still I shall never know, but my will did manage to triumph over my flesh. I should like the jury to give their fullest consideration to this point. I am sure they will.

We come then, at last, to the recordings themselves. I rather pride myself that, technically, they are really quite proficient, bearing in mind that I have no previous experience whatsoever in this field. I should very much like, when the court proceedings are concluded and my life has returned to normal to retain possession of the tapes for occasional viewing at home. I may even stand a television set on the kitchen table in Uncle Reginald's place so that I am able to view them at meal-times. I must confess to a certain fascination with the prospect of having the power to switch my uncle on or off at will. However, that is in the future. Now to the tapes. I shall not attempt to describe every detail of my little programmes. They are largely self-explanatory. I would, though, like to draw viewers' attention to various items of behaviour under each heading, these items being the ones (in my view) which most clearly demanded that my uncle should pay the ultimate penalty.

## 'BREAKFAST'

As you will observe, my recording of breakfast commences with what I believe is known as a wide-angle shot. This I arranged in order to capture the first teeth-jarring event in Uncle Reginald's daily performance. There is his empty chair and, behind it, the window that looks onto the back garden, and there, after a few seconds, is Uncle Reginald himself, taking his watch from a waistcoat pocket and checking it against the kitchen clock that I purchased by mail-order seventeen months ago. Now he sits down and places both hands, palms down, on the table. He blinks hard and deliberately three times, then looks around as if he had just woken up. At this point I always place a bowl of Weetabix with a scattering of bran over it in front of him. Notice how, as my hand appears on the screen, I lean forwards and smile into the camera secretly (a rather nice touch in my estimation).

Now, this is the moment of that first and quite sickening abomination. It occurs immediately after he has added milk and sugar very sparingly to his cereal. Oh, I can see it! I can see it! He clamps his hands to the edge of the table as if to obtain anchorage, and then it begins. A pendulum-like swinging motion of the buttocks over the surface of his chair, as though he were attempting to settle himself down into something wet and soft. It is a hideous movement of anticipatory relish, accompanied by a sound reminiscent of the sea sucking the tide back into itself on the beach, as he pulls air into his mouth through pursed lips, collecting dribbles and droplets of saliva from the front part of his mouth in the process. I have no doubt that you, viewer, whoever you are, are sensing as I have done so many times, the overwhelming pleasure and satisfaction with which one might take, say, the sugar bowl, and smash it with all one's strength into the face of a man who is guilty of such things! The skin of the aging buttocks, the wool of the underpants, the frayed nylon of the trouser seat, and the brown leather of the kitchen chair, they all move together, do they not? I might rest my case here and walk away a free man, but there is more. Yes, more!

## 'SUNDAY LUNCH'

For my Sunday lunch programme, I adjusted the controls on my camera so that it focused directly onto the spot where Uncle Reginald's plate would rest during the course of the meal. You will have already witnessed in the Breakfast tape the way in which he suspends his arms at an abnormal height above the food, his hands bending down at a full right angle from his wrists so that his knife and fork are practically in the vertical plane throughout the consumptive process. It reminds me of nothing so much as a Praying Mantis gobbling some disabled victim, the knife and fork being the probing, scraping ends of the long skinny front legs. Now, it was my intention to concentrate on the plate itself, and the horrendous manner in which my uncle dealt with the food thereon, particularly at the commencement and the conclusion of the meal.

The programme begins with a gratifyingly clear close-up picture of the hot food on Uncle Reginald's willow-pattern dinner-plate. You will note that this consists of three generous slabs of well-cooked beef, four quite substantial roast potatoes, a small pile of peas, a pair of golden-brown Yorkshire puddings, and three or four roast parsnips, all nestling in a shallow pool of thick brown gravy and accompanied on the extreme edge of the plate by a little splodge of horseradish sauce. Now, see how the extremities of my uncle's cutlery appear in the picture. They hover for a moment, then the knife descends. It moves the smallest potato approximately one centimetre away from its fellows and towards the peas. Why? Why has he moved it? There is no reason. It is gratuitous—it is offensive! It is only the beginning.

See now, how he executes two totally random rapid scraping movements with the prongs of his fork on a small portion of exposed china. Do not tell me that this is part of the business of eating. It is a symptom of contained excitement—of salivating, anticipatory greed. I know it! He impales a slice of beef with his fork and begins to cut. Cut, cut, cut, into little geometrically precise shapes, quadrilaterals that not infrequently aspire to genuine squareness. Now he pauses, the end of his knife dangling indecisively as he selects a vegetable. For no reason at all, he suddenly draws a Yorkshire pudding towards him for a distance that must be approaching an inch, then, with unbelievably crass indifference, pushes it back again. Why? The fork now pounces on a large fat potato and holds it firm while the knife saws its flesh. He is cutting it into cubes! God help us, he is cutting it into cubes!

So why—and this is the question that has burned through my very intestines during so many Sunday lunch-times in the last eight years—*why* does he then tear his Yorkshire puddings into ragged asymmetrical pieces using the *back* of his knife? What strange, twisted aberration can have been lodged in the mind of this person whom I called Uncle, that demanded millimetric precision with meat and vegetables, but a wild, formless approach to Yorkshire pudding? Something in his child-hood? Who knows! In any case, I am not one who differentiates between deliberate crime and psycho-logical disturbance. Evil is evil, and punishment is punishment.

The following phase in the preparation of Uncle Reginald's first mouthful of food is not for the squeamish. The fork selects a small square of beef, the knife pushes it crudely back to a lower point on the prongs, a cube of roast potato is added and suffers the same fate as the beef, two peas are affixed and subsequently totally penetrated by twin prongs, a previously shaped rectangle of parsnip is squeezed onto the now quite crowded fork head, and a smear of horse-radish sauce covers and semi-cements the whole. Finally, with a casual stab that, in my view, conceals a peculiar intensity of feeling, a long straggling piece of Yorkshire pudding is fastened to the very points of the fork prongs, and the mixture is transported up and out of the camera's view on its way to Uncle Reginald's mouth. Now, listen! That noise—that sound like wet lumps of meat going round in a washing-machine—that is him! That is Uncle Reginald chewing! And behind it, almost too quiet to be heard, but perfectly audible if one listens very hard, is the click. Yes! I have succeeded in actually recording the click. Hear it now. Chew—click! Chew—click! Chew—click! I hear it even in the silence of my cell, just as it can be heard on the tape. It is *so* clear.

The rest of my uncle's revolting activities require no further comment from me. The evidence is before you. Note one final point though, if you will. As the meal draws to a close, you will observe that I have left the table in order to widen the angle of the camera lens. This adjustment allows a perfect view of yet another significant piece of behaviour, one that cannot but impress the Court with the utter rationality of my decision to despatch the guilty one. See how Uncle Reginald continues his meal with un-abated and ghastly enthusiasm until only a small amount of food remains on his plate. Suddenly, as if out of breath, he lays his knife and fork down on either side of his plate, leans back, puffs his red, whiskery cheeks out, and expels air in a long whistling breath. Next, he places the palm of his left hand on his slight paunch and rubs it round in a clockwise direction, producing a low mooing sound of content-ment as he does so. That is hideous enough, but it is followed by an abrupt forward movement as he appears to notice, with a little shock, that he has not completely finished his meal. Picking up his knife and fork he pushes the remaining food into a heap in the middle of the plate, and is (apparently) just about to load it onto his fork when he changes his mind, lays his cutlery down in an exactly parallel fashion on the side of the plate, and in a bluff, genial voice, says the same three dreadful words that he has said at the end of the main course of Sunday lunch for the last ten years: 'An elegant sufficiency, eh? Ha, ha!' He *always* left a little food! He *always* said those words! How could he have failed to be aware of the fact that I *knew* every time, *every single time*, exactly what he was going to do and say? Of course he knew!

I was anxious that my uncle's execution should not be a painful one. The pursuit of justice does not require inhumanity, and I believe I am, in any case, a kindly person by nature. Accordingly, I spent some considerable time over the selection of an appropriate means of bringing about Uncle Reginald's death. Eventually I settled on simple asphyxiation with one of the spare pillows, and sentence was carried out (with rather surprising ease) on the Tuesday night following that final Sunday lunch. When Wednesday morning came, I made two phone calls. The first to Mr Robards to inform him that I was unlikely to be in a position to continue with my work for some little while, and the second to the local police station. I was, and am, aware that certain formalities will need to be observed before I am released, the most important of which is of course my trial. I might add, incidentally, that from the moment when the two policemen arrived on that Wednesday morning until the present day, I have experienced nothing but polite and caring treatment from all officials concerned. Indeed, I have positively enjoyed the experience of feeling, albeit in a minor sense, that I am by way of being a celebrity, the national newspapers having covered the story of my arrest and subsequent remand in some depth. My only regret is that the journalists involved in the writing of these stories have not had access to this document or to my two video tapes. If they had had such evidence available to them, there would not have been these constant references to 'pleas of insanity' and the like, nor would my name have been linked speculatively with famous 'murderers' of the past, people with whom I have absolutely *nothing* in common. However, the trial will make all things clear without doubt.

In the meantime I wait patiently, and look forward to the day when life resumes its old familiar pattern. Some things I miss. In particular the activity which for some time has constituted my sole form of recreation during the evenings and at weekends. At least once a week after work, and *every* Saturday afternoon, it has become my habit to hire a taxi to take me to Eastbourne. From there I catch the next available train to Victoria Station, and from there pass quickly down the outside steps to the underground station. After purchasing a forty-pence ticket, I follow the walkway to a point at which one can take a down-escalator to the Circle Line. I know no happier occupation than to travel on and on, round and round, on the Circle Line, observing people as they board and alight at each station. Why they should want to leave the train I really cannot imagine. It is wonderful to know that, again and again, you will return to the point where you started, and that there is no *need* to alight. It is with the greatest reluctance that I drag myself away on each occasion. Indeed, it has crossed my mind more than once recently, that the day might come in the not too distant future, when I may simply stay on the train, going round and round for ever, and *never* ever get off again.

# *Bethel*

BETWEEN BLACK CARN and Logan Rock lived a snail called Bethel, who became proud. Heaven frowns on a vain snail, and Bethel had become just a little too big for his shell.

Yes, one admired the polished chestnut brown of him, the pearly, whirly, swirling cream of him, and the pin-line midnight black of him.

And, oh yes, one was enchanted by the bright, intelligent eyes, ever alert on their majestic, grey, swaying stalks, eyes that were full of passion with just a hint of pain. Bethel's trail was broad and shining. He had loved and lost and learned and loved again. Always intensely, and always . . . slowly.

But a day came when poor Bethel, blinded by ambition, said rash things near French men, birds and children.

'I shall never be consumed on licensed premises.'

'I shall never be smashed into succulence on a thrush's stone.'

'I shall never be condemned to absent-minded death in a child's glass prison, on a pile of dead leaves, beneath holes that let air in but will not let me out.'

The world reacted.

A failed restaurateur named Dupin, a thrush with a past called Mulligan, and a fat-kneed child whose name was Wallace, formed a gang and, in a wooden shack behind St Levan's Church, swore an oath to crush the spirit—if not the life—out of brave, foolish Bethel who, in their hatred, they nicknamed 'Slugpot'.

The gang was armed and vicious.

Dupin carried an onion knife as long as his arm.

Mulligan had a leather quiver full of sharp, bright nails, hanging from a stoatskin belt around his neck. Dip'n'spit was his obsession. He could pin a butterfly to a tree-trunk from ten feet.

The child Wallace, carried a container shaped like a sneering face, into which he put things until they died. There was quite a lot in it.

The gang was very nasty indeed.

One day, Bethel chanced upon his own grave. The gang had done it to panic him, to soften him up for the kill.

Buried in the emerald dusk of a leafy wood near Trevilley was a small clearing. Here, beneath a notice-board fastened three feet above the ground to a young beech tree, two terrified lizards hacked frantically at the ground with silver cruet spoons, relics from some long-forgotten holidaymakers' picnic. Their small stupid mouths dropped open in horror as Bethel streamed easily into the glade, a favourite haunt—until now. By the sheer magnetism of his personality, he forced the trembling creatures to meet his steady gaze.

"Snot us, Gov,' jittered one, his eyes little black

beads of fear. A pulse jerked and jumped under the yellow skin at his throat.

'Froggy an' Frush an' Fatty made us done yore 'ole,' said the other desperately. 'We likes yer, don' we, Micky?'

'Said they'd scrush us impletely,' squealed the one called Micky, his whole spotted skin stretched with apprehension. 'Else bung us in Fatty's pot. So we adder dig yore 'ole, else. . . .' His shrill voice trailed off miserably.

But Bethel was no longer listening. He was reading the words that had been picked out on the notice-board in tiny silver nails. And as he read and understood, he no longer felt proud. He felt only fear.

IN BAD MEMORY OF SLUGPOT
REST IN PIECES
(. . . of shell. I ate the soft bit—signed, Mulligan).

Bethel felt the need for prayer and counsel. The hidden sanctuary in crumbling Penbar Cliff came to mind. A grinding journey for a pilgrim snail, but there, between the sky and sea, was a place of peace and meditation. There he could seek advice from fat old Mutton-cruncher, shrewd and kind, the last wolf in England. Converted years ago, the ex-carnivore worked out his penance as a minister to those in need, assisted by three white novice ewes who, protected by the depth of Mutton-cruncher's conversion and his complete lack of teeth, served silently and devotedly in the candle-lit depths of the Penbar Chapel cave. In the velvet hush of this holy place, Bethel, weary but strangely calm, prayed a simple prayer before he approached the wheezing pile of dog-collared darkness seated beside the altar.

The huge wolf's crimson tongue flashed out and

round and back as Bethel spoke with quiet urgency. The ancient yellow eyes snapped open for a startling moment, two tiny windows to the furnace of his brain. The snail waited, nervously sensing other, stranger supplicants in the deeper shadows of the cave behind him. He recalled strange tales of creatures so rare or ill-formed or wretched that the darkness of the cliff sanctuary offered the only safe home they would ever know.

At last the wolf stirred and spoke, his voice impossibly deep, unexpectedly warm.

'Are you brave and good, little snail?'

It was a time for truth.

'I have been proud. I fear for my life. I hate the gang . . . especially Wallace.'

What would Muttoncruncher suggest? What weapons? What strategies?

It seemed an age before the wolf spoke again.

'Have a party. Invite all three of them . . . especially Wallace.'

Bethel stared. Party? What did he mean?

The old grey head bent forwards. The wolf's last whispered words were for the snail's ears only. As he listened, Bethel nodded gravely. Soon, he turned to leave. The fear remained, but there was a new and better resolve in his heart.

Evening sunlight turned the dust into tiny specks of gold on Bethel's polished drift-wood desk, as the snail sat staring thoughtfully at three sealed envelopes propped in a row before him.

His home was a converted hip-bath at the bottom of a dried-up pond out towards Porth Loe. Bethel was not rich as molluscs go, but he was a lover of beautiful things. He had one of the best collections of blue china fragments in the whole peninsula, each piece neatly drilled with a small hole and suspended from the ceiling by a barely visible length of fishing line.

Then there was the quite unique framed set of dawn webs, somehow preserved intact with their original dew, just as they had appeared at the magical moment when the legendary joy spiders of Logan Rock completed their ecstatic morning dance.

Over the window hung a portrait of Bethel's maternal grandfather, Dicken, a great traveller who had been painted in oils by Salvador Dali. The great artist had later presented the finished work to Dicken in gratitude for a discreet personal service of unknown nature. It was a strange painting, but it meant a lot to Bethel.

It all meant a lot to him, this special place that had taken so long to find, furnish and make his own.

His eyes lingered fondly for a moment on his little personal library, a row of birch-bound volumes standing between two big pebble book-ends on the pine shelf beside him. He knew them all so well.

*I Dared to Call a Slug 'Friend',* the great liberal classic by Ambrose, the martyred pond snail.

*Is God a Gastropod,* the controversial best-seller of the sixties.

*The Whelk and the Spanish Dancer,* by an anonymous winkle.

And Bethel's favourite, *Out of My Shell,* a light-hearted call for freedom of expression by the Gwennap Head philosopher, Caliban.

All these things, the china, the webs, the picture, the books—they were all so dear and so familiar. Now, he was about to invite those whom he feared most in the world to come to his home for—of all things—a party! Would they not smash his home and all that was in it? Would they not smash him also? Glancing up at his grandfather's picture, he could almost hear old Dicken's careless chuckle: 'If a snail's got one foot in the grave, laddie he's *in* the grave!'

Bethel's heart nearly failed him. Only the memory of the wolf's head, dark and heavy beside his own, and the echo of the old minister's last whispered words, made him pick up the invitations and take them to the door where Micky the Lizard's youngest brother, Alf, was waiting to make the delivery to Dupin and Mulligan and Wallace.

Alf was very quick. Lizards had to be. It was their only talent, some claimed. A slow lizard was a useless lizard—a dispensable lizard. Alf hurried.

The first delivery took him up onto the St Buryan road where Dupin was busy in the greasy kitchen of *Le Cochon Mort,* a restaurant which an Egon Ronay agent had once described as 'La scum de la scum'. As a business it was dead, but Dupin was planning a private dinner for three. The invitation amused him. He spat into the milk pan and laughed in a gallic manner.

In his hollow oak armoury, Mulligan was sharpening nails with leisurely expertise on a flat, oddly discoloured stone. As he read Bethel's note, the expression of cold competence in his eyes did not alter in the slightest. He examined the point of a nail closely. It was not quite sharp enough.

Wallace was in his bedroom, squeezing super-glue onto the window-sill for sparrows. When his Aunt Pearl slid the invitation hastily under the door, he opened it slowly with his plump, raw sausage fingers, read it twice, licked his lips once, and glanced at the sneering pot in its special place beside the bed. His eyes gleamed, then disappeared as his fat face split into a smile. His lips moved silently, framing the word—'Slugpot'.

Every morning and evening, Bethel carefully filled the old brass oil-lamp that balanced on a bracket by his door. It was a matter of routine. It burned night and day. This evening, his head full of troubles, the snail had forgotten to carry out this small but essential task. In the very early hours of the following morning, the comfortable yellow flame flickered for a moment then, with a series of little popping sounds, died completely. Bethel, still wide awake with worry, went rigid with fear as the darkness slammed into him from all sides.

When snails panic they simply stop thinking. Bethel panicked badly now. It was the dark—he was terrified of the dark. As a very young mollusc there had been an unfortunate incident with a cockroach in the pitch-black bend of a wet and echoing drain-pipe. Little Bethel, exploring recklessly despite his mother's warnings, had cowered back into the angle of the drain as the huge glutted roach lurched heavily past chanting the same words again and again in a horribly flat, dead voice:

> Satisfied
> To rot inside,
> We eat and eat
> But don't excrete.

The loathsome creature hardly noticed the shivering snail. It was already far too bloated to bother with such a scrap.

Later, at home, Bethel's distraught mother had comforted the trembling podlet, while Grandpa Dicken, more than ready to take on the entire cockroach world single-handed, offered good advice: 'Roaches? Kick 'em in the legs— that's where their brains are!' Dicken knew a lot.

Nothing had ever removed the horror of the memory, though. Now, in the black silence, Bethel relived his childhood terror, and for an instant was unable to move. Then, like a crazy clockwork toy, he began to blunder from wall to wall, blindly seeking release from his own fear and from the army of phantom cockroaches that hunted him in the angry darkness. Things fell and smashed unheeded. Above his head, china pieces tinkled and jingled together as the whole house swayed and shook. At last the latch on the door was knocked loose and Bethel, feeling the flow of cool air on his body as the door swung open, turned instinctively in that direction, and was soon outside on the damp grass, his eyes drinking in the faint light from the cloudy night sky.

Those—and there are many—who label snails 'slow' should have seen Bethel that night as he urged himself, body and shell, up the grassy slope to the highest point of the cliff. There he rested beside a curiously shaped smooth stone slab, and, as if to reward his efforts, the moon, full and friendly, stepped from behind a cloud to illuminate the lonely cliff-top and the rock-strewn beach of Fool's Cove far beneath him.

Suddenly Bethel knew that all he wanted was escape from what awaited him on this day that had already begun—the party, the gang, the possibility of death. Never mind being good or brave—all that mattered was getting away. He looked up. The moon was very bright, the air as still as a sitting bird. Why should not tonight be the night for The Drop? It was early in the year. Usually he saved it up until late summer, but surely there would never be a night that was more ideal than this. The beach below was bathed in silver; in the far distance the ocean rumbled and whispered quietly in its sleep. It was perfect.

Excitement thrilled through Bethel's aching body

—the same excitement that possessed him every year just before the descent. In a fever of decision he levered up the flat stone beside him and dragged out the back-pack in its thick cellophane cover. No lizard on hand to help with the straps this year, but he managed somehow, and after a pause for breath he slipped over the tufted grass on the cliff-edge with a little gasp of exhilarated abandonment and felt himself falling like a stone through the breathless air.

'One—two—three—four—five!'

There was the familiar jolting tug at his body as Bethel pulled the rip-cord, and the parachute opened like a huge upside-down flower. That moment of blossoming safety seemed a special kind of miracle, and the dream-like experience of float-ing down in the moonlight was the most magical sensation he had ever known. But it was over *so* soon. Less than a minute later he was carefully adjusting the angle of his descent in order to land as near as possible to his destination. Seconds later he made a good landing on a small patch of wet sand, shrugged off his harness, and moved quickly towards the base of the cliff where a glowing patch of artificial light marked the position of Oscar Wild's Mollusc Repair Shop.

He passed the sign saying NO HERMIT CRABS HOW MANY TIMES DO I HAVE TO TELL YOU, and in the entrance to a natural cave, surrounded by tools, spares and general paraphernalia of his trade, he found the old mole busily burnishing a cockle by the light of a single electric bulb, powered by an ancient generator chattering away somewhere in the cave behind him.

Oscar was a well-spoken, rather classy old mole, who after years of small-time shell repair and synthetic slime production had seen his life and work revolutionized by the development of fibreglass. He was the best in the business and he could have become rich, but for some reason he chose to turn his back on financial gain to set up a workshop here at the bottom of the Fool's Cove cliff, where he served, serviced and repaired all manner of shelled creatures with great skill and discretion.

Bethel did The Drop once a year, partly for the obligatory slime and shell check, partly because he relished the whole experience, and partly because he enjoyed talking to old Oscar. The parachute had been Dicken's idea of course. Dicken and Oscar had enjoyed a very special friendship.

'How now, my brave Bethel?' greeted Oscar with a smile of surprise and pleasure. 'Early this year, are we not? How are we? Cracked, crinkled, crumpled, crushed? How goes it?'

'It goes not very well,' confessed Bethel as the cockle oozed away, and he climbed onto the work-pad. 'My big mouth really.'

He told the greying mole about the gang, the trip to Penbar Chapel, and the party that was due to begin in less than twelve hours, if it happened at all. Oscar nodded slowly as he tested a sliver of artificial shell against a small nick in Bethel's left side.

'Seen the wolf, have you? Ah!'

'Grampa Dicken always said I should visit Mutton-cruncher if things went seriously wrong,' explained Bethel, grimacing as the mole rocked him gently, listening for tell-tale creaks or rasps. 'So that's what I did.'

'Dicken. . .' Oscar chuckled richly at the mention of his old friend's name, 'Dicken never told you, I suppose, that it was the wolf's advice that brought me down here instead of—anything else?' There was a strange warm sadness in the mole's voice. 'And he was right. The wolf knows. Do what he says, you hear?' He patted the snail's shell affectionately. 'Off you go. You're finished, completed, repaired, mended. Pot of slime? No? Good to see you, little Bethel-Dicken. See you next year. Don't forget what I said now.'

A queue of claw-clicking, muttering creatures had built up behind Bethel. Much as he would have liked to talk more with Oscar, he knew that it was just not possible. Turning away from the warm glow and bustle of the repair shop, he saw in the distance Oscar's lizard gang folding and repacking the parachute. Before next summer they would have replaced it under its cliff-top stone. The system worked well. Nearby, Jacktar, the seedy middle-aged cormorant, was waiting to give Bethel his usual lift to the top. The overweight bird was just about able to flap that far. Not for the first time the snail wondered what kind of hold Oscar had over the black oily creature. Whatever it was, it certainly worked. A few unsteady minutes later, just as dawn arrived over the peninsula to chase the darkness into the west, Bethel arrived home safely, only to experience a shock of dismay on seeing the extent of the damage caused during his earlier panic. After filling and lighting the brass lamp, he wearily set about the task of restoring order among his precious things until, finally exhausted, he simply leaned his weight against a wall and slipped into unconsciousness.

For many hours his sleep was deep and dreamless, but eventually a dream did come, the strangest and most vivid nightmare that Bethel had ever had.

At first there was only mist—thick, yellow and chill, blotting out everything but itself. Bethel found himself in the midst of an alien, muffled world, listening intently and nervously as he waited for . . . what? He dared not move. Who could say what traps

and terrors were lying in wait behind the swirling
wall that surrounded him? He could not, in any
case, have moved more than an inch even if he had
wanted to. Wide leather straps were tightly criss-
crossed around his body and fastened at his back to
some kind of pole or stake. He shivered with fear
and cold in the menacing silence, knowing, as one
does in dreams, that someone or something was
coming for him—something bitter and cruel.

It began as a slight thickening of the mist directly
in front of him, gradually gaining substance until
Bethel became aware that a form of some kind was
making its way towards the spot where he had no
choice but to wait. Slowly the form began to take on
a definite shape—tall, thin, square-shouldered and
stooping, two little black eyes glinting malevolently
as the figure finally emerged from the mist and
stood over the terrified snail, its face wolfish with
grinning malice and triumph.

It was Micky the lizard. Taller, different somehow, full of an ugly sneering arrogance, but un-
doubtedly Micky. The long leathery body was
dressed in some kind of military officer's uniform,
with polished leather jackboots and a high-fronted
peaked cap. The grey material hung in baggy folds
around the lizard's scaly form. He looked all wrong
—like a skeleton in evening dress.

'You have two minutes left, snail. If you have not
told us what we need to know by then, you will be
shot.'

The creature's voice was high and grating, totally
confident, full of relish. Bethel's brain was spinning.
What was he supposed to tell them? Who were they?

'Micky, I. . . .'

'You will not call me Micky! You will call me "sir"!
Go on, say it! Say "sir"!'

The lizard raised a thin, vicious-looking swagger-stick above his head, his narrow face contorted with fury.

'Errr . . . sir,' said Bethel hurriedly, 'I—I can't quite remember what. . . .'

The creature lowered his arm, then bent from the waist until the smooth tip of his snout was almost touching the snail's face. As he spoke, a long twig-like tongue flickered to and fro, gently pricking Bethel's flesh each time it slithered out to its full extent.

'We want the French man and the thrush and the fat boy—especially we want the fat boy. Now that we have become the master race we intend to do to them what they did to us. We have suffered at their hands, now they will suffer at ours.'

The lizard's breath was hot and rancid on Bethel's face.

'We shall make the French man run errands for us on his hands and knees. Hundreds of little trifling messages and tasks all day and all night. If he stands up he will be shot. We shall make him go on and on way past the point where his skin is raw and bleeding. Eventually, we may cook him and serve him in his own nasty little restaurant with a nice green salad and a suitable French dressing.'

The tongue vibrated excitedly as the creature went on.

'As for the thrush . . . the thrush will never submit to our authority, nor will he show fear, but that will not matter. We shall imprison him in a large cage and use him for target practice. A moving target is useful—a fluttering one even better. We may invite the butterflies to join us. They too have suffered.'

Bethel very much did not want to hear what the lizards were planning for Wallace, but there was no escape. The harsh voice continued, tinged with the craziness that is fuelled by lust for revenge.

'We are going to be very, very fair with the fat boy. We shall do to him exactly what he has done to many of us. We shall pull his legs off to see if he grows some more—just out of interest, you understand?'

Snails do not go pale. They tremble. Bethel trembled now.

'But why. . .?'

'You know where they are, snail, and you are going to tell us immediately, or face the firing squad. The choice is yours.'

Bethel started to protest that he had no idea of the whereabouts of the gang, but stopped abruptly as it was borne in upon him that, in the context of this other dream world, he *did* know where Dupin and Mulligan and Wallace were hiding. He *knew*, somehow, that the three gang members were cowering abjectly in the attic of *Le Cochon Mort*, waiting for an opportunity to flee the peninsula. Assuming the lizard was to be trusted, he could free himself with a few simple words. And why not? He had no reason to love the evil trio—on the contrary. He would be perfectly justified in sacrificing them to save himself . . . surely?

'Very well!'

The creature stood up and drew back to one side. Behind the place where he had been standing the mist was beginning to disperse. Through the coiling wisps that remained, Bethel could now make out a tall wooden structure, supporting a platform on which a vaguely reptilian figure crouched behind a mounted gun of some kind. Stretching away from the corners of the tower to form a right angle, were two high metal fences topped with tangled masses of barbed-wire. Most chilling of all, though, was the line of a dozen lizards, uniformed and metal helmeted, who stood motionless, their rifles already raised and aimed at the very centre of the snail's body.

'You have until I count to five,' hissed the lizard officer, drawing a pistol from the holster on his belt as he spoke.

Five! Five seconds in which to decide whether to hand over the gang or not. An easy decision of course. Why should they live and he die? And yet. . . .

'. . . two, three, four—another second, my fine snail, and it will be too late. . . .'

Go on, Bethel, he screamed inwardly, tell them! Open your mouth and tell them, you stupid snail! In less than a second it will be too late!

BANG!

Bethel was woken by the sound of his door slamming, as Micky the lizard's brother, Alf, tried yet another ploy to wake the deeply sleeping snail.

'Gotta wake up,' insisted the lizard in a high-pitched nasal voice, ''snearly time fer the party! Gotta geddup—'sgettin' late. Gotta geddit all ready.'

From a sleeping nightmare into a waking one. Bethel stared at the hand-wringing creature for a moment, trying hard to focus on what had just happened, what was happening now, and what was going to happen this afternoon.

'I've goddall the stuff outside on the 'andcart like you said. Ice buns fer Fatty, seedcake fer Frush, an' onion rolls fer Frenchy. Got the drinks an' all. Dun good, din I?'

Bethel looked at the expression of quivering eagerness on Alf's face and remembered his dream.

'You've done extremely well, Alf. I had no right to ask you to do all that. You're very kind—thank you. Er. . . do you know what time it is? I invited them for about four o'clock, so—'

Alf was unable to answer for a moment, so shocked was he by the warmth and gratitude displayed by the snail. No lizard expected more than the odd word of curt approval. Pulling himself together he poked his head out of the door for a second and glanced up at the sun.

'Free twenty-free,' he called, 'eggsackly!'

'What?' Bethel was aghast. 'I've been asleep for hours and hours! Come on, Alf, let's get busy!'

'Right!' said Alf. 'Less get busy!'

By three fifty-five everything was done. Standing in a little group beside Bethel's house were three makeshift tables, each one laid with a member of the gang in mind. Alf's upturned cart bore a plate of onion rolls and a glass of wine for Dupin. A huge wild rhubarb leaf was anchored to a hillock by the seedcake, neatly sliced and laid out, together with a glass dish full of pure fresh water. That was for Mulligan. On Bethel's desk, dragged out of the hip-bath after a tremendous combined effort by the snail and the lizard, lay a plate of iced buns and tall glass of lemonade for Wallace.

'Whaffor you doin' this?'

Emboldened by Bethel's new attitude to him, Alf asked the obvious question. Bethel looked at him and slowly shook his head.

'I don't really know,' he said, 'I'm not sure. . . .'

Alf glanced meaningfully at his tail. 'Fink I'll be orf,' he twittered nervously, 'don' want Fatty ter see me.' He looked up. 'Free fifty-nine eggsackly—see yer later.'

Bethel waited alone by the tables, listening to the far murmur of the sea and wishing that he was as aggressively courageous as Grampa Dicken had been. A snatch of careless laughter made his heart race suddenly. They were here. Seconds later the gang appeared over the rim of the old pond, and

Bethel's heart, far from racing, nearly stopped altogether.

The next half hour was very strange. In a peculiar way it reminded the snail of Dali's painting of Dicken. Things were almost too vividly real to *be* real. And it was all so very quiet. The only thing that Bethel had said (in strangled tones) was 'Welcome. Th-thank you for coming. Please help yourselves to anything you—you want.' And the gang, without saying a word, had proceeded to do just that. As they ate they stared fixedly at Bethel, unpleasant anticipatory smiles on the faces of Dupin and Wallace, while Mulligan remained coldly expressionless.

They ate and drank everything on the tables. Every crumb. Every drop. Finally, Wallace wiped the back of a fat hand across his icing-smeared mouth and spoke for the first time.

'Party games now?' His little eyes glittered. 'What's inside?'

Mulligan ducked out of his leather strap, leaving the quiver of nails on the desk beside Wallace's sneering pot. 'I'll look,' he said shortly. He disappeared into the hip-bath, reappearing after a minute or so with a cluster of blue china fragments suspended from his beak by their lengths of fishing-line. He dropped them on the desk in front of the fat boy. Wallace picked one up and looked, first at it, then at Bethel.

'Pretty!' he sneered, then handed it to Dupin. 'Chuck 'em, Frenchy.'

Dupin laughed raucously. '*Oui, je les jetterai!*' he cried, and one by one he threw the pieces high into the air over the edge of the cliff and out of sight. Wallace beamed. Mulligan watched.

Snails do not cry. They slump, and their horns droop. Bethel knew that the gang were about to destroy his dearest possessions, bit by bit, enjoying every little flicker of response that could be elicited from their victim. He slumped and drooped. It was heartbreaking. Wallace dropped the framed webs onto a stone and Dupin ground the resultant mess into the mud with his heel. The picture of Dicken was propped up against Alf's cart and shredded by half a quiver of nails, spat with unerring accuracy by Mulligan from a distance of nearly ten feet. That was what finished Bethel off really—the clatter of heartless laughter as his only permanent reminder of Grampa Dicken was destroyed. It was too much. For the first time in many months, he withdrew into his shell and yearned for oblivion.

Resentment burned brightly in his soul. Why, oh *why* had he ever listened to what anyone else had said about what he should do? It was all very well for old Oscar and the wolf to give advice. They weren't about to be murdered after watching their most precious things being systematically demolished or thrown away. He could hear them out there now, those... those *cockroaches!* They were throwing stones at his house—heavy, mindless, denting stones. Soon it would be his turn to feel the keen edge of Dupin's knife, the agonizingly sharp points of Mulligan's nails, and whatever unspeakable torture the fat boy had in store for him. Alone in the clamping darkness of his own shell, Bethel felt as if his mind was slipping out of gear. As if in a fever dream, his head seemed to be thronged by a host of faces and voices from past and present, struggling and jostling to gain his attention. His own mother was there, pleading with him about something, but he couldn't quite hear what she was saying. Dicken, too, was urging him to act in a particular way, while old Oscar the mole just stared sadly at him from somewhere behind the others. There were other friends—and enemies, other sounds and voices. He wanted to turn his back on all of them—give up and simply sink into nothingness. If only they would let him.

Then, one face suddenly filled the space where all the others had been. One voice spoke quietly but clearly in his mind. It was the wolf, repeating the words he had whispered into Bethel's ear just before he left the Chapel cave. And now, for the first time, Bethel understood what he had to do, understood the strange dream of earlier, and understood that there was only one possible way for him. But he must do it now or it would be too late. Thrusting his head into the light, he cried out in a voice that echoed around the cliff-top like the notes of a golden trumpet: 'I forgive you! I forgive you! I forgive you!'

The effect was startling. Dupin, who had been advancing on the snail, knife in hand, turned a deathly white, let his weapon clatter to the ground, and turned and ran as though pursued by devils. Mulligan, who had just selected a spot from which to fire his deadly nails, rose abruptly on panic-stricken wings, and was very quickly just a dot in the pale sky to the east. Wallace was green and paralysed, his little fat mouth the only part of him that moved. It jabbered soundlessly. When he did finally stir, it was a backwards walk in slow motion. Slipping and stumbling, but apparently unwilling or unable to turn his back on Bethel, the flabby child retreated over the lip of the hollow, until even his fat green face bobbed out of sight, and a great silence fell over the cliff-top.

Behind the amazed snail, Muttoncruncher signalled to the line of grotesque and terrifying creatures whose heads had appeared above the edge of the dried-up pond as soon as Bethel's cry reached their ears. As silently as they had come, they left, to return to the sanctuary of the Penbar Chapel. By the time Bethel happened to look behind him, there was nothing to be seen.

But he had sensed the power.

# The Second Pint

As a teenager Flynn had hated Sundays. They offered him none of the things that he knew he wanted and believed he needed.

He wanted cafés, for instance, where he could sit and discuss life with friends and acquaintances in a cosy, hypothetical glow. In the little market town where he lived, only one café was open on the sabbath, and that was a place of dirty lino and clanking pin-tables, used with brutal exclusiveness by leather-jacketed bikers and a smattering of older men with crudely chopped hair and grubby personas whom Flynn had unconsciously classified as child molesting types. He was too fragile for all that; too frightened of facing his own dread of violence. He only really lived in his head, enjoying periodic conversational adventures in the clinking safety of chintzy tea-rooms.

Poor Flynn had never done anything except think and talk and smoke, but he had been quite an impressive sixteen-year-old for all that. Many of the contemporaries with whom he chatted in the Little Cottage Café on a Saturday morning (his favourite time) left, feeling that this untidy, faintly Irish person really did have a quite remarkable grip on the business of living. Little did they realize that even their most humble attempts to grapple with the realities of day-to-day problem solving were quite beyond the capabilities of Flynn, whose attractively pungent way of putting things was just the flashy label on an unspeakable can of worms.

Occasionally it would be a girl sitting on her own with him at one of the circular oak tables. He would be extra casual then. Girls terrifed him, but he had developed a number of self-titillating ploys which he was able to enjoy in absolute secrecy. Sometimes he would manipulate the talk round to the subject of art and then say with airy nonchalance, 'Of course, Picasso always maintains that he paints with his testicles.' The sort of girl that Flynn liked best would perform a perfect double-take, blush warmly, and do her utmost to match his nonchalance with a sophisticated nod and a half-smile of relaxed amuse-ment. 'Interesting and highly athletic,' he always added, looking as bored as possible, and inwardly relishing the intrusion of what he thought of as a grimy sex word into what he supposed was the freshness of her mind. Sex itself was out of the question. Far too horrendously, complicatedly close and real. All about skin and touching and giving and abandonment. Not Flynn's scene. Perhaps it would never happen—not outside his head anyway.

The other thing that Sunday lacked was an appro-priate number of people distracted by their own busyness. Flynn's favourite part of the week (other than Saturday morning) was Monday. No longer at school and unemployed himself, he knew no higher pleasure than that of setting out with a sufficient supply of cigarettes and money for a day's café dwelling, to stroll in a carefully nurtured trance-like state through streets peopled by busy workers and glazed-eyed housewives mentally listing and computing between shops. It was an intoxicatingly delicious sensation to be in, but not of the active world, to use the grey and granular backdrop of other people's daily grind as a means of finding colour and sharpness in his own image of himself. He moved and thought and felt in pockets and patterns of sensation-related place and time and environment, very defended, and very alone. Sundays left him stranded like a twitching fish on a beach, waiting for the tide of weekday ordinariness to turn and refloat him—to make him exist again.

When Flynn was seventeen he found a solution to the sabbath problem. He became a Christian. It began at eight o'clock one evening after a long and particularly bleak Sunday in autumn. He happened to walk past the open doors of a tall red-brick building set back from a small road which turned humbly off from the steep high street. People of his own age were going in, laughing and chattering in twos and threes. They looked clean and harmless. One of them noticed Flynn watching and invited him in. He went, unusually daring, and found himself in an after-church youth club where coffee and biscuits were served over a semi-circular bar set in a corner of the large church hall. He started to go every Sunday, becoming something of a group celebrity with his quick wit and carefully judged and controlled air of worldliness. Eventually, he started going to church until, in time, it was assumed that he had undergone some kind of conversion. He went away for weekend house parties with the rest of the youth group. He had views on things, and even occasional revelations. Sundays were transformed. Church-related activities and encounters provided a perfect filling for the Saturday-Monday sandwich. Was he really a Christian? Flynn didn't quite know, but it didn't matter. Sundays were all right now.

The years passed. Minor changes and adjustments became necessary in Flynn's life, but by the time he reached his forties, unmarried, living in another but similar town, and employed in an undemanding job which had altered very little over the years, he had established a pattern for Sundays, and Sunday evening in particular, which was as near perfect as he could imagine.

Every Sunday evening at six o'clock, for the last fifteen years, Flynn had put on clothes of a carefully average nature and walked the mile or so from his house to Portland Road, where two large and important buildings confronted each other on opposite sides of the street. That they were large buildings was an objective fact. That they were important was a matter of opinion. Flynn was unusual in that he was the only member of his church who used the pub, and, as far as he knew, the only pub regular who used the church. They had been twin habits of his for a long time now, and he had managed to extract considerable satisfaction from both environments, especially as he had consistently succeeded in keeping the whole thing well under control. He had always managed to escape real commitment to the church as a spiritual or a physical body (albeit sometimes by the skin of his teeth) and you could easily leave a pub if it looked as if you were going to be asked for something that you didn't want to give.

Altogether, it was a very comfortable arrangement for the head-locked Flynn. Into the church at six-thirty for an hour of stimulating and pleasantly dangerous observation of other people being vulnerable, then over to the pub at about seven forty-five to play, equally pleasantly, with the toy guilt that he allowed this to cause in him. He saw no reason why this should not have gone on indefinitely, but he was playing a very dangerous game, and one Sunday things went badly wrong.

The church which Flynn attended was a very lively one. People sang loud joyful choruses as though they really meant the words. Some put their arms in the air as they sang, others held their hands out in front of them, palms upward, a few even danced on the spot or, more freely, out in the centre aisle. Prayer time was long and intense, sometimes involving the use of spiritual gifts such as 'speaking in tongues', or prophecy. All of the prayers were extempore and heartfelt in tone; frequently a member of the congregation would start to weep and be surrounded by a little knot of elders or sympathizers laying a hand each on the sufferer, and praying him or, more usually, her through to a release from grief. The sermon, or 'message' as it was called, tended to be far longer than one would expect in the more traditional churches and was almost always related in some way to the themes of repentance and salvation. Communion was called 'coming to the Lord's table', and happened every other Sunday. It was a central event in the lives of the people in Flynn's church, but they used cherry-ade instead of wine, so as not to offend those whose consciences were troubled by alcohol, or tempt folk who had problems with restraint in that area.

Flynn used the church and its members as he had used them since that night more than twenty years ago when he wandered into the red-brick building in his home town. He was able to be vivid and significant among people who were predominantly mild and anxious to be good, and it was safe in an edgy sort of way. Inside him two strands of response had remained unaltered throughout the years. One was a dull, unspecific yearning, the other a rigorously maintained and largely defensive cynicism. The two ran parallel like live wires. Flynn knew that they must never touch. There had been dangerous moments, chances, invitations, opportunities, but they had all passed without him being shocked out of himself.

On the Sunday in question the service was led by Maurice Daniels, a large, energetic, boy-like man, whose talents lay more in the areas of organization and practical application than in encouragement and exhortation to worship. Flynn knew that Maurice always experienced a little crisis of confidence at about the midway point of the service and that he invariably perceived this as a problem in the congregation rather than in himself. The big man's equilibrium could only be restored (so Flynn's observer's logic told him) by something blatantly spiritual happening among those whom he was supposed to be leading. Today was no exception. Halfway through 'He is Lord', Maurice signalled to the musicians to stop, and addressed the congregation in a low, but confident voice, only his eyes dancing a little with the fear of failure.

'I sense that there's a spirit of heaviness in the room,' he intoned, his mouth very close to the microphone. 'I think the Lord would have us open our hearts and spirits to him and each other for healing this morning.'

There were two or three 'amens' and a loud 'hallelujah' in response to this. Flynn mentally rehearsed certain well-used procedures in preparation for what was about to come. Encouraged by the verbal assent to his diagnosis of the problem,

Maurice went on, his eyes steady now.

'We will sing that chorus through twice again, and as we sing, if you feel you need ministry, just catch the eye of a brother or sister nearby and they'll come and pray with you.'

He signalled once more to the musicians. Piano, violin, guitar and metallophone swung into mellow action again, but more quietly this time. Maurice raised one hand high in the air above his head as he led the singing.

Flynn had two alternative coping ploys for situations like this. One was the eyes-shut-praying-for-others ploy. Simple but effective, all it involved was sitting with a straight back, eyes lightly closed, with a small smile of faithful serenity to indicate that no ministry was needed *here*. The other was only possible when the words of a relatively uncommon chorus were displayed on the overhead projector screen. Then, Flynn would peer fixedly at the screen, apparently too concentrated on the unfamiliar words to be concerned with catching or being caught by anyone else's eye. That one would be useless today. Everyone knew 'He is Lord' by heart. It would have to be the closed eyes and seraphic smile. Above all, don't look around, don't risk a glance in any direction at all. Flynn had become an expert in the art of avoidance. Perhaps he had become a little too confident in his techniques, because now, in the infinitesimal moment between the commencement of the chorus and the lowering of his eyelids, he knew that an almost non-existent engagement of the eyes had occurred between himself and Arnold Fuller, one of the most fervent and devoted members of the congregation. Alone in the darkness, he knew that Arnold would be upon him in seconds. He braced himself. It wasn't the first time. It wouldn't be the last. He could handle it. He had handled it before.

'Bless you, brother. Let me pray for you.'

Arnold had come round behind Flynn so that he could lay his hands on his shoulders. He was leaning forwards and speaking right into the left ear of his needy brother.

'I saw you looking at me, my friend. I think the Lord is going to do something really wonderful for you tonight.'

Flynn clenched everything and concentrated on his voice. He knew he could manage his voice.

'That's great, Arnold. I don't know what it's all about, but it's always good to be prayed for.'

He was a master of the defusing response, but it didn't work this time. Arnold was starting to pray, and he was doing it quite loudly.

'Lord, I believe you want to really break into this life tonight, in a completely new way. I just know that your Holy Spirit is waiting to fill our brother with all the love and joy and peace that you promise to those who follow you, and that's what we're praying for right now!'

To his horror Flynn, his eyes still closed, heard the scraping of chairs as others got up to assist Arnold. A hand was laid on his head, an arm was placed around his shoulders, someone in front of him was holding both of his hands, fingers rested on his knee. The music had stopped. Flynn was in the centre. Arnold's voice rose a gear as he went on praying.

'O Lord! I really believe that you are going to release your child from bondage this night! That you are wanting to do a mighty work of redemption in this man's life! Break down the barriers, Lord, and just let your Spirit have his way with our brother! Oh, hallelujah!'

Arnold and several others started to pray in

tongues, and the hands resting on various parts of Flynn's body pressed and quivered with powerful intention.

Inside his head, Flynn was shouting and screaming and panicking and pleading and longing and hating and arguing. Outside, he continued to smile quietly and acceptingly. He had still not had sex with anyone. He was not skilled with passion. All this was forcing him to feel extravagantly. He might burst into tears. He would hate that. They would like it. Good sign. He might shake them all off, stand up and shout obscenities, then rush from the church into the wonderful open air. Very soon those parallel wires were going to touch and then anything could happen. If he could just hold on a little longer, just a little longer. . . .

'Amen! Thank you, Lord!'

Arnold leaned forward to whisper in Flynn's ear again.

'Okay, brother?'

Flynn's warm smile and gentle patting of Arnold's hand as it rested on his shoulder was absolutely perfect. Costly, but perfect.

'Thanks, Arnold—really appreciate it, brother.'

Everyone sat down again and the service continued. Maurice swung his arm exultantly as he conducted the opening verse of 'Bind us together'. There was an atmosphere of joy and achievement.

Flynn was a pallid, sweaty, trembling wreck, but he looked fine as he joined in with the singing. For some reason, difficult to define, he comforted himself inwardly with his knowledge that the last few minutes were solely a product of Maurice's insecurity, Arnold's need for spiritual excitement, and the congregation's tendency to follow like sheep. He could see through Maurice and Arnold—and the rest of them. He could see under people's skins.

Others couldn't. He could. That's all there was to it.

But Flynn was shaken. He had always been very careful not to be drawn in any real way into what he saw as the carefully organized spontaneity of the services, but for once he had not been vigilant enough. He had been lucky to escape with as little attention as he had, but there was still the possibility that they would get him in the social period after the service was over. Luckily, he was sitting at the back, near the door, always the safest place to be in any church, Flynn reckoned. As soon as the last prayer had been said, and the roll and clack of the kitchen hatch heralded coffee time, he did a back-in-a-minute walk through the door, and headed straight for the pub.

He needed time and beer. Lots of time to recuperate from this disturbing experience, and lots of beer to assist any necessary process of self-justification, or if that didn't work, to provide the courage not to care.

It was beginning to get dark outside. He shivered slightly as he crossed the road to his other habit, the Britannia Arms, a majestic Edwardian establishment whose massive landlord, Edgar, served perfect beer to Christians and pagans without discrimination, or indeed, any apparent interest. He employed a number of minions who did bob and smile and hurry around, but they only served to highlight his huge indifference to the world in general and customers in particular. It was the perfect place to recover and chew over his sins, but—there was a problem. The Britannia had three bars, two large and one small. Flynn hesitated outside the pub for some minutes, knowing that whichever bar he chose, would, with the consistency of natural law, contain Trev.

Trev was an elderly alcoholic whose life revolved

around the maintenance of his status as a regular at the Britannia. Actually, he was more than a regular. He was a constant. Trev was *always* there, smiling, winking, ready and willing to advise Flynn on any aspect of his life that, in Trev's opinion, needed attention. Flynn was diseased with politeness in certain relationships, and had allowed the old man to feel that he saw him as a sort of wise elder, without whose words of wisdom he would never dare to make any major decision. Flynn was fond of him in his own limited way, but it was a curious fact that whenever he particularly didn't want to see Trev, he was invariably ensconced in the bar that Flynn decided to use. It was rather like the old magician's trick with the three cups and a ball. Flynn never managed to guess right. Sometimes he tried to cheat fate. He would approach the saloon bar at speed, veer sharply to the left at the last moment, and crash through the door of the Snug, to the considerable alarm of all those present, except, of course, Trev, who would wave and smile as usual in happy anticipation of another counselling session with his inadequate friend.

Today, Flynn didn't want to talk to Trev. There was something so appallingly real about the defeat and decay behind the old alcoholic's pub brightness. Flynn knew it would prevent him from moving smoothly towards an enjoyment of his own problems. He decided to opt for the saloon bar, usually the quietest part of the pub. Tonight was no exception. There was only one other customer. Sitting in an armchair in front of the imitation coal fire beneath a huge picture of the Queen, Trev lovingly caressed his early evening pint of mild, and gestured invitingly at the chair beside him. Accepting defeat, Flynn closed the door behind him. One of the minions supplied him with a pint of old ale, and soon he was settled comfortably by the fire, anticipating with relish the familiar illusion that the beer, defying gravity, was draining upwards through his brain, putting out all the little fires of tension and guilt.

'All right,' said Trev, wiping his mouth with the back of his hand. 'What's up?'

Flynn took another mouthful of beer without answering. He was feeling better already.

'Lets 'ave some nuts,' suggested Trev. 'Dry roast. Then we'll sort you out.' He leaned back and smiled benignly. 'I'll gettem if you like.'

Flynn sighed as he heaved himself out of his chair and returned to the bar. It was one of the sacred traditions of their relationship that he never accepted any offer from Trev to buy him anything. The unspoken understanding was that Trev's contribution of wisdom and guidance was worth far more than Flynn's humble offering of beer and nuts. In any case, Trev's slender finances were organized down to the last half pint necessary to remain a bona fide customer at the Britannia for the whole of the week.

'Let me get you another pint as well, Trev. Same again?'

Flynn quite enjoyed this bit usually. Trev's brows would knit and his mouth would drop slightly, as though his companion had made some totally novel suggestion. Then his face would clear, and he would smile wonderingly, as though fascinated by his own response to a unique invitation.

'Jew know, I honestly think I will,' said Trev, sounding like someone who has lost a battle with his principles for the first time. 'Yes, I will!' The decision was made.

For Flynn, there was something very special about the second pint. He was invariably awash and at sea after the fourth or fifth, but the second represented that point at which he was committed to neither sobriety nor drunkenness. He was neither innocent nor guilty. Part of him could swear that there would not be a third. Another part knew with purring assurance that there would. All was well. All was peace. Morality slept. It was a beautiful but neutral pint, the second one. If, in addition, there was a little pile of dry-roast peanut dust in front of him, ideal for consumption by means of a wet forefinger, then, for a short time, the world could not hurt him, and God could only frown, fold his arms, and tap his foot. All of them—man, God, spirits of the air, denizens of the deep—all were obliged to suspend operations while Flynn finished his second pint. All, that is, except Trev.

'Why jew go to that church?'

Flynn was stunned. It was a question that really meant something. He was so used to Trev's wholly predictable, half-baked philosophy that he was temporarily incapable of answering. Despite his curse of politeness, he had always known that he was really only humouring this sad old alky. Now, with one deft step, Trev had arrived at the centre of his immediate inner life, and Flynn had to decide whether to kick him out or not. He stalled.

'What do you mean, Trev? Why does anyone go to church?' Panic filled him. It was as though something had pursued him across the road.

'Them at your church, an' me. Little beggar at playin' games, aincher? Playin' games with us. Them an' me. Aincher?'

This was awful! Had Trev gone completely mad? Had he forgotten that he was just a broken-down alcoholic and Flynn wasn't? Didn't he know that Flynn secretly despised him; that he could switch him on or off in his life like a television programme?

Good grief, the man seemed to be getting the idea that he existed! What did he mean, 'Them an' me?' What could Trev and the people at church possibly have in common? Playing games? The eyes of Flynn's mind narrowed. There was no way he was going to get turned over again this evening. He had no words. He surveyed all the possible avenues of escape, and rejected the honourable ones. Beer would do it. Trev's geniality could be bought back with more beer. A bottle for the baby—something like that. Flynn laughed lightly as he stood up.

'You're in a funny old mood, Trev. Let me get you another pint. Cheer you up.'

Battle raged in the rheumy old eyes, but after a few seconds it looked as if Flynn had won. Trev's swan song as a genuinely involved human being was cut short—extinguished—by a single pint of beer. He licked his lips, swallowed hard, and twisted his face into a fair imitation of the old familiar grin. He said nothing, just nodded and slapped his hand down on the arm of his chair. Time enough later, Flynn thought, for profound regret, self-criticism, and all that. Right now, he felt only relief that, once again, he had found a way to safety.

Turning away from the fire, he jumped a little as he saw that Edgar, the landlord, was watching impassively from behind the bar. The huge man said nothing as he served the beer, but there was a stillness in his gaze that left Flynn feeling vaguely uneasy as he made his way back with the drinks.

He had some difficulty fitting two more pint glasses onto the shiny surface of the little wrought-iron table that stood between them. He was still only half-way through his second pint, and Trev had only just finished his first. But never mind. The panic was over, and it was comforting to see the glasses of dark brown liquid nestling together, winking and gleam-

ing in time with the repetitive patterns of light
thrown out by the flames of the artificial fire.

'Cheers, Trev.' As Flynn drew the other half of his
neglected second pint fondly towards him, he
glanced up at the old man's face. Oh, no! He was
crying! Two large tears were rolling down his face,
his eyes blinking furiously as he fought back whatever was trying to come out. A few sniffs later he
seemed more or less all right, and after a couple of
explosions into a big off-white piece of cloth
dragged from the side pocket of his crumpled
jacket, he sat quite quietly for a minute or so, gazing
into the fire.

Flynn? Verbal paralysis. He finished his second
pint.

'I'm saved, yer know.' Trev's hands trembled
slightly as they rested flat on his knees. For the time
being he seemed to have forgotten his beer.
'Salvation Army. Just 'fore the war. Saved in the
street, I was. Saved for Jesus.' His right hand rose an
inch or two, and swung gently from side to side,
perhaps conducting some dimly remembered gospel tune from the past.

Flynn put the empty glass down softly on the
table, and picked up his third pint. Trev saved? He
didn't look very saved. He looked lost. Old and lost.
He was intrigued. Now that the pressure was off he
could afford to be interested. He had a number of
scintillating insights into this particular topic, and he
was more interested in impressing the old man than
he had been before. He snuggled back into his chair
and addressed the other man lightly and reasonably,
waving his right hand occasionally to emphazise a
word.

'All right, Trev, granted that all those years ago
you did have some kind of conversion experience—
and don't get me wrong, I'm not saying you didn't—

but. . . .'

'To hell with yer buts!' The old man turned on Flynn, his face working with anger and some kind of ancient frustration. 'You listen ter me! One day 'e's gonna pick me up an' dust me down an' look straight in my face an' say, "Trev, you're an old soak, an' you ain't never done nothin' fer me, all you've done is get drunk, an' sleep—but Trev, mate, you—are—saved!" An' you—' Trev suddenly stuck his arm out towards Flynn and wagged his finger in his face. 'You'll get *spat out*, because you ain't even a soak. Fish nor fowl, you ain't. You ain't nothin'!'

He stood up, shaking with emotion, and without taking his eyes from Flynn's, picked up the pint he had just been bought, and half dropped, half threw it against the stone surround of the fireplace. There was glass and beer everywhere, and a fierce hissing as the liquid penetrated to the heat source of the fire, sending a cloud of steam up around Trev's angry figure as he leaned forwards to deliver his final speech.

'I'm gonna drink a lot more beer tonight, but I ain't drinkin' that one!'

It was another nightmare. Flynn sat through this outburst, quite unable to move, helpless as ever in the face of raw emotion, and especially violence. It was a relief to hear the calm, determined tones of the landlord breaking into the silence that followed the old chap's last words. He spoke from somewhere just behind Flynn.

'I'm not having this. Come on, you. Out!'

Poor old Trev. Flynn felt what he supposed must be a genuine twinge of sympathy at the thought of the old man being thrown out of his beloved local, but he felt so shaken up by what had happened, that he couldn't help looking forward to being able to relax when he'd gone. Trev was still standing, the top half of his body bent forwards, his eyes glaring into Flynn's. He didn't seem to have registered Edgar's words at all. Flynn tried to be kind.

'Come on, Trev. No point making trouble. Best if you just go really. What d'you think?'

Flynn's heart leaped with shock as a heavy hand landed from behind on his shoulder, and Edgar's voice, slow and sure, sounded once more.

'I'm not talking to Trev, I'm talking to you. Out!'

Flynn hadn't even started his third pint. He passed through the door in a daze, and stood for a few moments, quite terrified, gnashing his teeth in the outer darkness.

# Except Ye Become. . .

(A LITTLE GIRL *runs up to a very satisfyingly*
*policemanish sort of policeman.*)

GIRL: *(Very breathless.)* 'Scuse me . . . oh, 'scuse me
. . . Mr Policeman . . . Sir . . . 'scuse me!

PC: 'Allo, 'allo, 'allo. What's all this then, young
feller-me-lad?

GIRL: I'm a girl! And I've found a flower.

PC: *(Laughs.)* You've found a flower, 'ave yer? I see.
Well that's 'ardly a matter for 'er Majesty's police
force now, is it?

GIRL: But you don't understand. It's not an ordinary
flower—it's . . . it's . . . it's beautiful and it's tall
and it's special and . . . please come and look!

PC: Well . . . I don't know . . .

GIRL: *(Rustles a paper bag.)* I'll give you a rhubarb and
custard sweet if you do.

PC: Bribing a police officer, eh? All right then, just a
quick look.

GIRL: It's over here. Come on!

PC: All right, all right. *(They move to the flower, looking up.)* Well, blow me down!

GIRL: Don't you think it's lovely? I think it's lovely. Do you think it's lovely? I think it's—

PC: *(Interrupts worriedly.)* Oh, it's er ... lovely all right, but I am bound to point out in my official capacity that *(firmly)* it can't stop 'ere. Lovely and all that it may be, but it's blockin' the path and is therefore what we in the police force term a public nuisance. If it 'ad 'ad the sense to grow four feet away, over there, it might—I say might—'ave been all right. Apart from that, it's too blinkin' big!

GIRL: *(Aghast.)* Too blinkin' big for what?

PC: Well ... it's obvious isn't it? It ... well, you imagine one of them petals falling off and 'itting someone on the 'ead. Besides, you'll 'ave everyone walking along 'ere with their 'eads in the air not looking where they're going, and before you know where you are they'll be crashing into each other all over the place.

GIRL: Please ... you can't hurt it. It's too—

PC: Let's 'ave a look at the old rule book. 'Ere we are. *(Clears throat.)* Section thirty-six, paragraph twelve, line eight. "On encountering strange, abnormal or obstructive growths, the officer present shall summon a detachment of 'er majesty's armed forces, horticultural division, with three long blasts of his official whistle. He shall then relinquish 'is post to the military officer in charge." Right! 'Ere goes! *(Blows whistle three times. Army squad enters—one officer and two men.)*

HIGGINS: Left, right, left, right. Halt!

PC: Ah! That was quick. Now, as you can see, *(laboriously)* we 'ave a case 'ere of what you might call—

OFFICER: *(Interrupting briskly.)* All right, Constable, carry on. The army is here now, we'll handle things. Where's the flower? Ah, yes. Right, men. I don't know what it is, and I don't understand it, so I think we'd better blow it up. The enemy are devilish cunning, and I think what they've faced us with here is an unexploded flower. Corporal Higgins!

HIGGINS: Sah!

OFFICER: When I give the word you will place a small explosive charge at the base of the suspected object. Detonation of said charge will cause said device to explode, thus rendering said device harmless to the general public.

HIGGINS: Sah!

OFFICER: Private Hoggins!

HOGGINS: Sah!

OFFICER: Clear the area of all civilians until the danger's over. Shoot any who resist.

HOGGINS: Sah!

OFFICER: Right, men. Move!

HOGGINS: Right . . . back . . . back. . . . Move along if you please, sir. . . . Now, what have we here? . . . I'm sorry, miss, but you can't stop here. (*Rising impatience.*) We have a job to do, miss, and that involves you moving right away from that . . . that flower. Will you let go of it? Right, if that's your attitude. . . . 'Mission to speak, sah!

OFFICER: Carry on, man.

HOGGINS: Sah! This person, sah! Refuses to move, sah!

OFFICER: I don't think you understand the danger you're in, miss. When that thing goes up, it'll take you with it.

GIRL: But it's a flower, not a bomb . . . and even if it is a bomb, it's beautiful and frightening. You're ugly and frightening. Can't you please leave it alone?

OFFICER: Her mind's gone, Hoggins. Hold her back

till we've finished.

HOGGINS: Sah! Right—you heard the officer— *(shouts)* Move!

GIRL: Ow! Let go! I think you're all horrid!

OFFICER: Right. Everybody down! Ready, Higgins?

HIGGINS: Sah!

OFFICER: Ignite on the word of command. Ignite! *(Small explosion.)*

GIRL: *(Running joyfully to the flower.)* It wasn't a bomb! It wasn't a bomb! You see! You see, sir! It wasn't a bomb! The flower's still there!

OFFICER: When you grow up, little girl, you'll hear about something called logic. If the army says that an object is a dangerous explosive device, and steps are then taken to destroy the device, then logically said device can no longer exist. I see no flower. Do you see a flower, Higgins?

HIGGINS: No, sah!

OFFICER: Hoggins?

HOGGINS: No, sah!

GIRL: But it is still there. It is isn't it? You can see it, can't you? Oh, do look! *(The soldiers prepare to move away.)*

OFFICER: Right, men—let's move!

HIGGINS: Left, right, left, right. . . . *(Fades into distance.)*

*(Fade in to news.)*

NEWS-READER: Here is the news. In the heated debate in the Commons tonight, Mr James Bland, the Minister for the Environment, sought to give assurances to the opposition spokesman on horticultural affairs that the large flower which has recently appeared in a small provincial town does not constitute a serious threat to national security. Mr Bland said that although contingency plans did exist for dealing with such a crisis on a national level, he had no reason to believe that the local authority concerned was not fully competent to deal with the situation, and that interference by central government in local affairs was not a feature of the manifesto that had brought his party to power. At the same time, he added, the government was fully up to date on the crisis and prepared to intervene if and when it became necessary. Replying to suggestions that the troops had in fact already tried and failed to subdue the flower, Mr Bland said that he was unable to comment for reasons of security. Meanwhile, observers report that the flower continues to flourish.

Now, the Middle East conflict, and after this week's fresh outbreak of hostilities. . . . *(Fade out. Fade in—stirring, insistent documentary music is heard—to the introduction to the TV programme* Focus.)

PRESENTER: Good evening and welcome to *Focus*. Once again we are zooming in on a subject of current national concern. Our aim as always is to reveal the truth behind the rumours, to ask the important questions, and, if possible, to provide some of the answers. Tonight—it's the flower problem. Not flowers in general, but one flower in particular: the flower which stands behind me here. In a very short space of time this 'growth from below the ground' has threatened to undermine the very fabric of our society. Why has a single flower, admittedly an unusual one, given rise to so much controversy and debate? The alleged failure of the armed forces to deal with the situation raises serious questions about internal security, and indirectly the effectiveness of the present government. Should the flower go, or should it stay? People everywhere are demanding an answer.

Tonight, we have invited four experts to join us here on the spot—a comparative horticulturalist, a cabinet minister, a minister of the church, and a child psychologist—to give us their ideas on the implications of, and possible solutions to, this pressing problem. We are hoping—everyone is hoping—for some answers here tonight. But, first of all, could our children be in danger? For an answer to this question we turn to a child psychologist, Miss Olga Fink.

PSYCH.: I would like to say straightaway that I believe this flower to be a serious threat to the healthy mental development of those children who encounter it, and there are good reasons for this belief. I think everyone would agree that the flower is abnormal in many ways. For the developing child an encounter with such abnormality can grossly disturb and disrupt that perception of an ordered world which is so necessary to the maturing infant, and in some cases could cause serious damage. We can only achieve real security by seeing ourselves as units in a world where the laws of nature and human behaviour have never, and will never be, altered to any great extent. Clearly, then, the child who is suddenly exposed to such a phenomenon as this absurdity will begin to develop the dangerous notion that *(dramatic pause)* ... things do not necessarily have to remain as they are. Throughout his life that child would be expecting, perhaps in serious cases, even hoping, for something more than the real world has to offer. Such an outlook can only lead to fantasy, depression and a paranoiac dissatisfaction with life as it really is. If we persist in allowing our children's minds to be filled with false ideals, they may become as obsessive as this child here, who originally found the flower and now seems hopelessly ensnared by the mutation. Unless I'm very much mistaken her responses will already be heavily conditioned by exposure to this plant. Let me show you what I mean. *(Approaches little girl as though visiting a dying relative.)* Little girl, what do you think about this flower? What do you see there?

GIRL: *(Puzzled.)* A flower.

PSYCH.: *(Indulgently.)* Of course, yes . . . but I mean, how does it make you feel inside?

GIRL: Happy.

PSYCH.: Happy?

GIRL: Yes, happy.

PSYCH.: Happy? Happy? *(Annoyed.)* What is happy? I want to know why you keep staring at this . . . thing.

GIRL: Because . . . it's beautiful. It's just . . . beautiful. I just love looking at it—it's *so* beautiful.

PSYCH.: But . . . *(Gives up in despair.)* As I thought, this sad little girl is already almost incapable of rational conversation. She sees only what appears before her, her feelings are dictated by her emotions, and her thinking is governed almost entirely by her thoughts. To use an old-fashioned term, she is . . . simple. If this flower can have this effect in so short a time, we *must* decide how best to protect our children in the future. In my view, there can be no doubt—the flower must go!

PRESENTER: A grave warning indeed, and one which I am sure will cause parents everywhere to ask of the authorities, 'What are you going to do? What is the official view of the situation?' To answer these questions we have with us tonight the minister for the environment, the Right Honourable James Bland. Minister . . .

BLAND: Well, I think everyone will agree that there has already been too much beating about the bush on this issue. The time has come for somebody to make a committed stand on one side or the other. There has been quite enough talk—more than enough discussion. What is needed is the courage to put forward a definite viewpoint and stand by that viewpoint, whatever the consequences.

The flower must go! So say those who take that particular line, and I am in full agreement with any action which ensures that such an option remains a viable alternative. The arguments put forward in favour of preserving this plant are equalled in potency only by the highly respected views of those who do not take that particular stance. Let us not consider personal feelings, except to the extent that they guide us to a solution based on certain facts which must be ignored if the truth is to be served. The government is quite clear on this issue. We intend to pursue a firm policy of action until that policy is rendered obsolete by virtue of its inability to fulfil those objectives which caused it to be put forward in the first place. This kind of consistency, involving as it does a healthy refusal to equate theory with mere practice, will result in the flower staying within the boundaries of a situation which is defined by its insistence on a strong decision concerning the removal of restrictions on the flower's ultimate fate. Our position, then, is clear. We both oppose and support resistance to measures which are exclusive of either side of the argument. To those who do not welcome this kind of straight talking, we simply say, 'Leave it to those who do.' Thank you.

PRESENTER: Well I don't know what our viewers made of that, but I'd like to ask you a straight question, Mr Bland. Are you in favour of removing the flower, or allowing it to stay?

BLAND: That is exactly our position, yes.

PRESENTER: I'm sorry, Mr Bland, but can I press you a little further on that? What is the government going to do? What are your immediate plans? Where do you go from here?

BLAND: *(Pause.)* To the station. So sorry. Train to catch, must run, so sorry. All under control. . . . *(Fades into distance.)*

PRESENTER: Well—so much for the government view. That was Mr James Bland, minister for the environment. Now, let's turn to the church for the spiritual angle, and I want to ask the Reverend William Cuthbert, vicar of the local church, how he sees the situation. Reverend, what do you think of this flower?

REVEREND: I must start by saying that I have personally examined this flower very carefully, and I have no hesitation in saying that it is one of the most beautiful things I have ever seen. The flower is, in fact, so stimulating *(a dangerous word for him?)* that I think it must be approached with care. The effect of such a bloom on both children and adults is very difficult to predict.

PRESENTER: What should we do?

REVEREND: I believe that a period of waiting is indicated. In, let us say, ten years time, it should be more possible to assess the implications of this lovely object and perhaps even to give the go-ahead for free and general enjoyment of such unusual beauty.

PRESENTER: And in the meantime?

REVEREND: My suggestion is that the flower should certainly *not* be destroyed. Rather, let the church remove the plant and keep it carefully during the next decade in a secure part of one of our church gardens where it can neither harm nor be harmed, as might be the case if it were left out here in the open. At the end of that period the situation could be reviewed and the whole matter reconsidered.

PRESENTER: And in the meantime the flower would not be on view at all?

REVEREND: I am sure the church would have no objection to selected groups viewing the flower with the co-operation of the clergy involved. To this end one could prepare a viewing rota which might be concentrated on weekends, and also include one or two periods during the week.

PRESENTER: So what would the next move be?

REVEREND: I think that our priority must be to remove this beautiful thing from general circulation, both for its own safety and for the safety of those who may falsely interpret its meaning. We cannot be hasty in these matters. We may, *(pauses as he becomes increasingly absorbed by the flower)* like this little girl, feel ... greatly attracted in a very simple way to the sheer loveliness of the flower, but perhaps in a sense *(comes to his senses)* she has started at the wrong end. We have a wonderful thing here. Let us not spoil it by relying too hastily on our initial responses to what we see. We have made one or two mistakes of this kind in the past. The result has been division, argument and disharmony. I hope that we have now learned our lesson. *(Increasing in confidence.)* We need to develop a universally accepted system of formal appreciation with regard to this flower before we allow passion or excitement to cloud the issue.

PRESENTER: Thank you very much, Reverend. Miss Fink, what do you think of the vicar's suggestion? Do you agree with him?

PSYCH.: Oh yes. If the flower is taken over by the church I think we can all stop worrying. It will be forgotten within weeks.

PRESENTER: Well, we seem to have an uneasy agreement there. Now, before we turn to our last speaker, I'll see if I can get a comment from the little girl who first found the flower. *(Goes to her.)* Hello, there! All the people listening would like to know what you think about this flower. Would you like to tell everybody?

GIRL: *(Pause.)* I think . . . I think . . . it's so lovely. I can't think of anything else to say.

PRESENTER: Okay, well now, you've listened to what all these people have been saying about what should be done with the flower. What do you think we should do with it?

GIRL: I think . . . perhaps . . . we should water it and then look at it some more.

PRESENTER: *(Touched.)* We should water it. I see. All right, you go and get some water while we go on with our programme. *(Girl leaves.)*

GIRL: All right, but you will look after it, won't you?

PRESENTER: Yes, yes of course. *(Turns to camera.)* If only it was that easy, but it's not. So let's turn to our last expert, Doctor Harry Winter, an internationally known comparative horticulturalist who has done much to bring horticulture to the people in a way that can be accepted and understood even by those who find it difficult to appreciate flowers of any kind. Doctor Winter. . . .

WINTER: Right, if we could just gather round the flower. Good. Thank you. Well, you know, I think this whole thing has got rather out of hand, and I want to show you how a proper horticultural perspective will invalidate most of the myths which seem to surround this so-called flower. The fact is that in a very real sense, this flower simply cannot exist. It goes against all we know about plant growth. Let me say categorically that this is *not* a new species of plant. I've seen it all before. Everybody screams, 'New flower, new flower!' and within a few days it turns out to be artificial or poisonous or freakish. This growth cannot exist in any known type of soil or climatic condition, and it will certainly never reproduce itself. And yet some people, including myself, do not feel that the flower should be totally destroyed. It has a certain ... potential ... charm, and I believe that any qualities that this plant possesses should be available to everybody. I suggest, therefore, that we preserve the flower, but in an acceptable form, in a form that will allow people to say, 'Yes! This is something I can enjoy without having to abandon my common sense.' Let me show what I mean. *(He produces a pair of garden shears and prepares to cut.)*

REVEREND: Are you sure that.... *(Sound of first cut.)* Oh dear!

WINTER: If I just snip off this branch here ... and this one.... Cut a little more off this side.... Now, let's shape these petals ... and again.... *(Lots of vigorous snips.)* There! I think that deals rather neatly with the situation. The flower now conforms to normal expectations, it can no longer harm the minds of little children, nor can it exhaust the wits of our politicians.

PRESENTER: Well, there we are. The flower problem seems to be a problem no more. Thank you, Mr Winter, Miss Fink, Reverend Cuthbert, and thank you for joining us. From *Focus*, goodnight.

*(Everybody leaves except the vicar.)*

PSYCH.: Are you coming, Vicar?

REVEREND: Er, no ... I think I'll just wait for ... that is wait until ... oh dear, oh dear, oh dear!

*(The little girl arrives back with her water.)*

GIRL: I've got the water . . . I . . . oh . . . oh no! *(Pause.)* Oh look, look at your poor, poor petals! Oh, I'm so sorry.

*(Silence.)*

REVEREND: I'm afraid we . . . I didn't think they'd actually hurt it. *(Pause.)* I wish . . . I wish I could have stopped them. I just didn't have the courage, I'm afraid. *(Pause.)* Do take your head out of your hands. Please don't cry.

GIRL: *(Raising her head.)* I'm not crying.

REVEREND: Oh. . .?

GIRL: I'm remembering.

REVEREND: Remembering. . .?

GIRL: My flower. I thought someone might do something to it, so I looked and looked and looked at it so that I'd remember every bit of it.

REVEREND: And do you . . . remember every bit of it?

GIRL: Yes. I do. Every bit.

REVEREND: Hmmm . . . I'm afraid that although I remember it was very beautiful, the details are rather hazy. What with all the speakers and the discussions and . . . well. *(Pause.)* I wish I could see it again.

GIRL: Well. . . .

REVEREND: Yes?

GIRL: I could tell you about it.

REVEREND: Would you? Please.

GIRL: Well, it was tall, and very unusual, and very, very pretty—and the colours—they were . . . they were blue and red and yellow. They were the best thing. . . . *(They walk away hand in hand.)*

## Marl Pit

I'VE ALWAYS RATHER resisted the idea that one should go grubbing about in the past hoping to find something that will help to explain the present. Perhaps I don't think enough about things like that. I don't know. My life has always seemed quite happy enough without all this close examination of one's own entrails that seems to happen so much these days. My wife laughs at me and says I'm plain vanilla to everyone else's raspberry ripple, and I wouldn't know a complex if one batted me round the ear. She's probably right. I'm an uncomplicated sort of character. Fond of the family, keen on work, love my pipe—that sort of thing.

I've never seen any sense in the suggestion that none of us are anything like we appear to be. You know the sort of thing: 'He's so noisy and confident. I'm sure he must be a very shy man. . . .' Load of rubbish if you ask me, but that's how a lot of people go on. If you can prove he was in love with his teddy bear when he was two, they say, that will explain why he can't bring himself to play shove-halfpenny with left-handed Welshmen now that he's forty. That sort of thing's not for me and never has been. Why, I can't remember much about last week, let alone things that happened when I was a child. Sufficient unto the whatsit is the thingummybob thereof, I've always said. My son's the same—sleeps like a baby (he's sixteen), gets up with a smile, strolls through the day doing this and that, yawns a bit when it gets late, goes to bed, head on the pillow, fast asleep in seconds. Just like me.

Now, the reason I say all this is to show just how unusual it was for me to suddenly remember every detail of that one particular day twenty-seven years ago, when I was about nine and a daily attender at the little junior school up on the other side of the common near our village. It was my wife who triggered the memories off at breakfast one morning. She looked up from the paper and said, 'You lived in Natcham when you were a kid, didn't you?'

'Yes,' I said, 'we were there until I was about eleven. Why—what about it?'

She looked down at the paper again and tapped one of the columns with her finger. 'There's a bit here about a court case, and one of the men—the defendants—comes from Natcham. Might be more than one Natcham, I s'pose. Here—you have a look. I'll start clearing up.'

I wasn't wildly interested, but I read the article with time-consuming care to give my wife and son plenty of opportunity to clear the breakfast things and wash them up without my valuable assistance.

The piece in the paper was about a criminal trial involving four men who were accused of brutally assaulting an elderly night watchman in the course of a major robbery. It appeared that the injuries inflicted on the old man were way out of proportion to what would have been needed to keep him quiet. The prosecution described the attack as 'vicious and bestial'. It was a horrible story, and I wasn't very anxious to dwell on it, nor was the name of the Natcham dweller very significant at first. His name was Duncan Tapman, age thirty-six, the same as me. It wasn't until I'd laid the newspaper aside after much over-elaborate straightening and refolding, that the whole thing hit me. Duncan Tapman! Of *course* I remembered Duncan Tapman, although I hadn't thought about him for years and years. And with the return of that memory came a whole set of other memories, all connected with a wet Friday in late autumn when I was a not very confident junior, and Duncan Tapman was. . . .

'Well?' My wife suspended sink duties for a moment. 'Ring any bells?'

I was feeling a bit shocked. I knew that I needed to take this flow of memories that had fountained up from nowhere into my mind, and carry them carefully, like the contents of a brimming beaker, to a quiet place where I could safely examine them. There was nothing to say to anyone else about it until I'd done that.

'Mmm . . . maybe. I'm not sure.'

Later that morning I set out to drive up the motorway to visit a friend in hospital in Northampton. It was ideal. Time and space to find out why the recognition of that name earlier on had been accompanied by such a sharp stab of guilt. Something to do with that Friday. An almost unbearably pungent flow of emotions passed through me as faces and scenes from the past appeared with extraordinary clarity in my mind. Who was our teacher at the time? I could see her perfectly, but her name escaped me for the moment. She'd been very thin

with a scraggy neck and black hair caught up somehow at the back. Impossible to say how old she was.
All adults were 'about fifty' when I was a junior. But
I didn't like her. There was no doubt about that. I
didn't like her at all. I remembered how powerful
she had seemed. Grim and powerful, glaring down
from a desk at the front that seemed to my childlike
eyes a good ten feet higher than the regimented
rows of sloping desks at which we sat. I remembered
wondering in a private, embarrassed sort of way,
whether Miss Duncannon might be a variety of
witch. Duncannon! Of course! She was called Miss
Duncannon, and her fingernails were so long that
she could reach out and poke a boy sitting right at
the back of the class without even getting up from
her desk at the front. I laughed aloud at the absurdity of this non-memory, a sort of impressionist
memory I supposed. Because she *was* like that. She
could control and punish and disturb any boy in the
class without effort. She was an expert.

Pulling out to overtake one of those drivers who
seem to need a slow slow lane, I remembered that
the Friday in question had started with one of those
demonstrations of total control. A boy called Roger
Burn had swung his satchel carelessly as he came in
that morning, and accidentally torn a section of the
new 'frieze', a wall decoration that the whole class
had been working on every day for the past week.
There had been loud cries of 'Oh, Roger!' followed
by the much more ominous 'You wait till Miss
Duncannon sees that!'

We all waited with considerable relish to see what
Miss Duncannon would say when she saw 'that'. She
never disappointed the more bloodthirsty element
in the class. This morning was no exception. I was
reading my brother's copy of *The Eagle* when she
swept in and took up her customary stance behind

the teacher's desk, her beak of a nose impaling our spirits to her will as it travelled slowly through a one hundred and eighty degree arc. We were all on our feet by then, of course, including the wretched Roger whose cheeks had turned to the colour of raw pastry as he awaited his fate.

'Good morning, class.'

Her voice was resonant, unmarried, business-like.

'Good morning, Miss Duncannon.'

We performed the usual chanted greeting with mechanical rectitude.

'Sit!'

We sat.

'Answer your names as I call them—Ablett, Arnold, Atwood, Avingdon, Bance, Benson, Burn, Crowhurst. . . .'

Roger's 'Present, miss' had been an unintelligible, strangled bleat.

'Volume, Roger!'

We knew that this meant 'say it again, but louder'.

'Present, miss.'

An intelligible bleat this time. The register proceeded.

Anyone who could have overheard me as I motored up the M1 that morning would have been bound to conclude that I had mislaid my marbles with a vengeance. I went through that twenty-seven-year-old register two or three times at the top of my voice, filling in gaps each time, until I was fairly sure that I had total recall of the list of names. It fascinated me that all that information had been pigeon-holed somewhere in the back of my mind for all those years. I shook my head slowly in wonder as I drove.

'Does anyone have anything they would like to tell us?'

That had been Miss Duncannon's next question.

She always asked it. We were allowed five minutes
each morning to broadcast information about ourselves to the rest of the class. Naturally, we did this
in the only really meaningful way at play-time and
on the way home from school when there were no
grown-ups about, but Miss Duncannon insisted on
the daily formal exchange and woe betide us as a
class if one or two of us didn't squeeze out a sick
grandmother or a new bike. Perhaps we would
rather do sums or copy out from the board, Miss
Duncannon would suggest, if no one was concerned
enough about others to let them know what was
happening in our lives. Very recently deceased
relatives were especially popular with all of us,
including Miss Duncannon, and, if I remember
rightly, the bereaved class member as well in most
cases. Miss Duncannon would deliver a soberly dramatic little lecture on how John or Michael or
Frankie would be feeling sad and upset today, and
how we must be specially thoughtful and careful
with them between now and going-home time. John
or Michael or Frankie would then move through the
day in a sort of physical and verbal slow motion,
exhibiting the fragility that was expected of them
and postponing any real grief until they had
enjoyed their suddenly acquired celebrity status.

There had been no dead relatives on that Friday,
but there had been a torn frieze which, as headline
news, was easily on a par with a death in the family.

'Please, miss. . . .'

It was Richard Arnold, the class sneak. He was
very useful to us. We could hate him for telling tales
and hiss imprecations at him afterwards, but we
needed him to trigger off the X-rated scenes of
pedagogic vengeance and chastisement that were so
awesome and so enjoyable.

'Yes, Richard?' said Miss Duncannon, melting

infinitesimally. 'What do you want to tell us?'

Roger Burn sat two desks away from me. His mouth was drooping open and he was blinking very hard every few seconds. All I remember thinking was what a wonderful stroke of luck it was to not be Roger Burn.

'Please, miss, Roger tore our frieze that we done. He tore it with his satchel when he came in this mornin'.'

Everyone sat up a little straighter, folded arms a little tighter. You could have cut the silence with a guillotine. Miss Duncannon studied the place on the wall near the back of the classroom where part of the frieze hung limply, its jagged edge indicating that this was the scene of the crime. Then she looked at Roger, her eyes like little black bullets.

'Well, Roger Burn, I think there's something we ought to say!'

If ever anyone needed a script in a hurry it was Roger Burn that morning. I could see his mouth twitching soundlessly as he desperately sought a form of words that would spring this hideous trap that he found himself in. I knew exactly what he was thinking. He was thinking that whatever he said would turn out to be evidence of his callous indifference to others. If he just said he was sorry, Miss Duncannon would reply that sorry doesn't get friezes mended. If he said it was just an accident, Miss Duncannon would say that she might just have to smack his hand accidentally with a ruler for being so thoughtless. If by some miracle he was able to convey coherently that he was very sorry about accidentally damaging the frieze that everyone had worked so hard on, and that he would repair it at his own expense and in his own time as carefully as he possibly could, then Miss Duncannon would say that that was all very well, but wouldn't it have been much better if it hadn't happened in the first place. Roger was in a no-win situation, and he knew it.

'We're all waiting, Roger! What are we waiting for you to say?'

'Don't know, miss.'

A delighted, shock-filled, air-trembling silence.

'You've just damaged a piece of work that has taken us all week to finish, and you don't know what to say? Is that possible? I'm very sorry to find that you have no feelings at all about what you've done.'

No one looking at Roger at that moment, pale and quivering with confusion and dread, could possibly have seriously claimed that he had no feelings at all about what he'd done, but his internal mechanism was stuck on 'don't know', and none of us were about to argue the point with the teacher.

'I'm still waiting, Roger Burn, and I do not intend to wait much longer! Now, what do you say?'

Roger reminded me of a baby bird I'd once seen, cornered by a cat, its heart hammering frantically against its chest, quite unable to move or make any sound other than a terrified little chirp.

'Don't know, miss.'

'Well, little master don't know. . . .'

We giggled obediently.

'I'm going to give you one more chance to find out that you do know! Everyone else knows, don't you, class?'

One or two hands shot up towards the ceiling, but Miss Duncannon wasn't interested in hearing from anyone else. She quelled them with a tiny gesture.

'What am I waiting to hear you say, Roger Burn? And this is the last chance you get!'

Roger's life seemed to have escaped through his open mouth. All that was left were those three hoarsely spoken words.

'Don't know, miss.'

I found myself jabbing the accelerator of my car in anger at the memory of what happened next.

Miss Duncannon went icy cold and just stared at Roger for a few seconds, then she spoke in a dry, deceptively casual voice.

'Come out to the front, Roger, and face the class.'

He stumbled his way to the front and stood facing us. He looked like the sort of suet pudding that you have to throw away in the end. I thought how sad my mother would be if it was me out there, and she could see me. I hated Miss Duncannon and I wished it wasn't all so exciting.

'Well now, class. Here's a boy who doesn't know. Whatever you ask him, all he can say is that he doesn't know. But why doesn't he know? The answer must be that he doesn't know because he's a fool. So what you see standing in front of you here is a fool whose name is Roger. Are you a fool, Roger?'

Roger's face wasn't white any more. It was deep crimson.

'No, miss.'

Miss Duncannon left her desk and walked forward until she was standing beside her helpless victim. She bent forward from the waist and spoke right into the side of Roger's face.

'So you've discovered something you do know, have you? Well, I don't agree with you. I think you are a fool, and I'm going to prove it. Do you think I can prove it?'

'N-yes . . . don't know, miss.'

'Go and bang your head against that wall, Roger— over there by the door.'

Hesitantly, Roger, still bright red in the face, walked stiffly over to the yellow-painted wall and stood for a moment with his forehead resting against the plaster.

'That's it,' coaxed Miss Duncannon as though

humouring a lunatic, 'bang it against there a few times. Off you go.'

Like some sick-at-heart animal performing a foolish trick, Roger banged his head against the wall three times, then looked back at his teacher.

'Roger,' she said quietly.

'Yes, miss?'

'Only a fool would go and bang his head against the wall when he's told to. Go and sit down.'

Quite a lot of children laughed of course, as she knew they would. She really was an expert. Some smiled. *I* smiled, mostly out of fear. I didn't want to be next.

Duncan Tapman didn't laugh or smile. His place was the one between mine and Roger's, and I noticed that as Miss Duncannon returned to her desk, his face was set and angry and his left hand, the one nearest me, was clenched so tightly that the knuckles looked bloodless. It frightened me a little.

Duncan Tapman. . . .

As I moved out of my lane onto the approach road to the Newport Pagnell services in search of coffee, I thought about Duncan Tapman. By the time I was seated with my drink in the midst of the bustling cafeteria, it had all come back to me.

Duncan Tapman's face had been closed up in a way that, as a child, I never really understood. It was as though there were bruises right inside his head that were so tender that if he relaxed his face the pain would be unbearable. There was a pronounced puffiness around his eyes as well, although actually his face (like the rest of him) was bony and tough looking. I knew him, at that time, simply as one of the two roughest boys in the school. He lived in a rough road, he did rough things, and he used rough words, not, as we did, with deliciously conscious wickedness, but naturally and casually. He never came to tea at our houses and we didn't ask him to play with us. He was outside. He didn't belong. He wasn't like us. He had a strange solitary independence which we didn't understand, like one of those grim-faced gunfighters on the films who won't hurt you as long as you don't get in their way. We were rather scared of him, I suppose.

I wasn't the only one who had noticed Duncan's clenched fist. Miss Duncannon missed nothing. Her eagle eyes were fixed on that left hand of his as it rested, quite still, on the desk in front of him.

'What have you got in your hand, Duncan?'

'I 'aven't got. . . .'

I was close enough to Duncan to see what happened next, although for a while I wasn't sure what it meant. He had obviously been about to unclench his fist and show Miss Duncannon that there was nothing in it, when a strange little light appeared in his narrow eyes and the whole of him seemed to relax slightly. Instead of opening his hand, he just loosened his fist a little so that it looked as if he could be holding something about the size of a ping-pong ball. He spoke again, quite politely.

'I 'aven't got nothing in my 'and, miss.'

I'm sure Miss Duncannon realized that this boy was never going to bang his head against a wall just because someone told him to, but she was quite capable of varying her methods to suit individual cases.

'I can put up with a great many things, Duncan, but I cannot stand a liar. I shall ask you once more. What are you holding in your hand?'

The atmosphere was electric. No one had been expecting a second feature, least of all one involving the enigmatic Duncan.

'I'm not 'olding anything in my 'and, and I'm not a liar, miss.'

Duncan drew his closed hand towards his chest as though guarding its contents from attack. Miss Duncannon nodded twice, slowly, her thin lips compressed with anger. But she must have felt she was on very solid ground. Why had the boy not simply opened his fist if he had nothing to hide? She drew herself up very straight. In an old book about the First World War at home, I'd got a picture of a judge putting on the black cap before sentencing Sir Roger Casement to death for treason. If Miss Duncannon had had a black cap available now, I was sure she would have put it on.

'What is the punishment for lying in this class, Duncan?'

'Cane, miss.'

'Correct! So if you persist in telling me untruths, you know what your punishment will be.'

Her voice rose into terrifying gear.

'Perhaps you think that one fool in this room is not sufficient. I think you must believe that I am as great a fool as Roger. Is that what you believe?'

'I 'aven't got nothing in my 'and, and I'm not lying, miss.'

Duncan covered his fist protectively with the other hand.

Miss Duncannon was really angry now, but still well in control. She took her cane from its two supporting hooks on the wall, her eyes never leaving Duncan in case he dropped 'it' while her back was turned. Laying the length of bamboo with cruel delicacy on the front of her desk, she sat down and beckoned with one skinny forefinger.

'Come up to my desk, Duncan. That's it—now stand beside me here so that everyone can see you. Now, you still say that there's nothing in your hand?'

Duncan paused for the barest fraction of a second, as though debating inwardly whether to own up or not, then, still cradling his fist to his chest, answered as politely as before.

'Yes, miss. There's nothing in my 'and, and I'm not tellin' lies.'

'Very well!'

Miss Duncannon shot a hand out and grabbed Duncan's left wrist, pulling it towards her and twisting it so that when his hand opened, everyone would be able to see what was inside.

'Now, class,' she said, 'I'm going to make Duncan open his hand in front of you all. If there's something in there, then he's a liar and I shall cane him, but if there is nothing in there'—she spoke with dry, totally assured irony—'then I am a fool and Duncan had better take over as teacher.'

Reaching round with her other arm, she prised Duncan's fingers open to reveal a completely empty hand.

For Miss Duncannon it must have been as if the sun had set in the east. She remained quite motionless for a few seconds, while her face seemed to turn a yellowish colour. You could see her going over in her mind the words she had just said. A ripple—largely of unease—passed through the class. We may not have been very keen on Miss Duncannon, but there was something uncomfortably off-centre about what had just happened.

'Can I go and sit down again please, miss?' asked Duncan quietly.

Miss Duncannon seemed to come to with a start. She looked with narrow speculation at Duncan for a moment, then spoke with dismissive briskness as she released his wrist.

'Yes, Duncan, go and sit down. We've wasted quite enough time already this morning. Sit up straight, class! Let's see how well we know our seven times table.'

It was a fine retrieving performance, and most of the class hardly realized what had happened. I knew, though, and Roger Burn knew judging by the little smile on his face, and I'm quite sure Miss Duncannon knew what had really occurred.

Duncan had punished her for what she had done to Roger.

I glanced at my watch. Lost in the intensity of my memories I hadn't noticed the time was passing. Swallowing the cold remains of my coffee with a grimace, I hurried out to the car and was soon 'burning rubber' as my son puts it. I didn't allow my thoughts to return to Duncan Tapman and the other significant event of that Friday until much later in the day after I had visited Jeanette. My visit followed the usual pattern. A long, chatty walk through the beautiful grounds of the mental hospital, lunch at the restaurant that catered for patients and their friends, and the usual tearful farewell at the door of Jeanette's unit. She was an old friend of ours—very sick—and we were all she had really. I promised we would all come up for a day in the spring.

Motoring back that afternoon I found that my thoughts about Jeanette and her situation drove me back almost irresistibly to my memories of earlier in the day and the event which must have had a lot to do with that moment of guilt I'd experienced on first recognizing Duncan's name in the newspaper.

The rest of that Friday had been fairly uneventful as far as school was concerned. It was too wet for us to play out after dinner and at play-times, so we were all pretty lively by the time we escaped Miss Duncannon's care and popped out of school like a succession of little corks from a bottle. I set off to walk home over the common with Roger Burn, who had fully recovered from his ordeal of the morning, and my other best friend, Michael Atwood, who sat directly behind me in class and lived two roads down from me in the village. These friends of mine were deeply, vitally important to me. In fact, at that time, they were probably *the* most important thing in my life. Being alive was about having friends, doing things with friends, working out ways to keep friends, and, sometimes, learning how to cope with being hurt by friends. That didn't happen very often, and it was probably unintentional and meaningless when it did happen, but it always knocked the bottom out of my world for a short time, and revealed a soft, emotional part of me that was occasionally responsible for slightly bizarre emotional outbursts. One of them happened on this damp, chilly, autumn afternoon, and it was all because of what these friends of mine did to my school cap.

We all wore caps—green and yellow ones—at our school. As far as I could remember they were always either too big, or too small, or if you did find that yours fitted, it probably didn't belong to you anyway. It was as much a part of life as Dan Dare and six-of-chips that, every now and then, your cap would be snatched from your head by a friend or foe and carried gleefully to a safe jeering distance. That left you with the choice of employing 'chase and kill' tactics, which was exactly what the snatcher hoped you would do, or trying to give the impression (not easy for your average healthy junior) that the whole thing left you too bored for words. Either way you usually got your cap back in the end, or if not your cap, a cap. My mother never seemed to mind too much if I ended up with headgear that wasn't strictly my own, as long as it was in as good or better condition than the one I started off with. In my time I'd both suffered and inflicted this tra-

ditional schoolboy insult many times, but on this particular afternoon I felt it had got rather out of hand.

As we reached the village end of the common,
Roger, who was rather hysterically high spirited
after quitting the scene of his earlier ignominy,
grabbed my cap from the back of my head and ran
off holding it high in the air, making Red Indian
noises by wobbling his finger in his mouth as he
went. This didn't trouble me too much, but when we
rounded the next bend in the path, he was waiting
by the edge of the dank and reedy pond that
everyone called the Marl Pit. Goodness knows what
it had been originally, but over the years it had been
used by the local people for dumping all their un-
wanted rubbish, and now it was a foul smelling ex-
panse of black water with the legendary bottomless
centre so beloved of schoolboys and tourists
everywhere.

Roger waited until I was inches away, then, with a
shrill whoop, he drew his arm back and flung the
cap as far as he could towards the centre of the
pond. Michael laughed, of course—so did I. It was
more than your life was worth to look upset. But
already my mind was racing with dismal questions.
How on earth would I get the silly thing back? What
would my mother say if I went home with no cap at
all? I wasn't supposed to go anywhere near the Marl
Pit anyway. If I waded in and somehow avoided
drowning, then went home soaked to the skin, my
mum would kill me. If I didn't wade in and went
home capless, she'd kill me even more.

My friends had started to shy stones and mud at
the green and yellow target as it lay flat on the
surface, supported by reeds or rubbish just under
the water. They made noises like artillery shells as
they lobbed their ammunition. They were having a
great time.

For me it had become one of the coldest and most miserable afternoons I had ever known. Retribution awaited me at home whatever happened, and here were these so-called friends of mine setting out with great relish and enthusiasm to make things as bad as they could by sinking my headwear. As a large clod of grass and earth plunketed heavily into the target area, to the accompaniment of loud cheers from Roger and Michael, I started to cry deep down in my stomach. It was a technique I'd learned early on in junior school to avoid the humiliation of crying real, wet, visible tears. There was no acceptable nine-year-old vocabulary for the feelings I wanted to express at that moment, but I could feel, rising up from inside me, the tear-laden, retardedly deep voice of that other hurt child who seemed to inhabit me at times like this: 'You're supposed to be my friends.' They loved this, of course, and the target practice continued with even greater vigour and much delighted laughter at my expense.

Several other boys, heading homeward, were passing our noisy group by the pond. One of them, taller and thinner than the rest, had left the path and come over to see what all the fuss was about. It was Duncan Tapman.

Duncan had heard my ludicrous appeal for mercy. He didn't laugh. He stood, hands in his pockets, quite still except for his eyes, looking with growing awareness from me to my friends, to my cap, and back to me. Then our eyes met. It was a moment of genuine identification. I suppose that for once, and on a level that was quite indefinable, we were equals in suffering. All of a sudden he raced off in the direction of his house, calling out that he'd be back in a minute. Five minutes later he galloped back wearing an enormous pair of rubber boots. Without saying anything he waded out towards the centre of the evil smelling pond and, reaching forwards, as far as he could, retrieved the soggy lump of cloth that my cap had become. Splashing his way doggedly back to the bank, he threw it carelessly at my feet.

The peculiar desolation that always crept over the common at the end of those chill, dripping days in late autumn, was beginning to spread through the atmosphere as I bent and picked up the cap. Duncan, apparently quite unconcerned about my response to his good deed, had picked up a long whippy stick and was tapping it rhythmically against his leg as he stared out over the dark stretch of water, whistling softly to himself. My friends, unwilling to risk a challenge to this cool customer, had already forgotten the entertainment of the last half hour and were turning towards where the village lights burned richly in the dusk on the edge of the common, only minutes away.

But I had to get things sorted out before I got home that evening. I needed some definite sign or symbol that my friends were still my friends. I was a rather old-fashioned child in a way, I suppose. As Michael and Roger started to move away from the pond I barred their way and extended my hand stiffly and formally.

'Shake hands? No hard feelings?'

This odd, unnecessary gesture embarrassed and amused them, but they did shake hands. Perhaps, for a second, they realized how important it was to me.

So everything was all right.

I glowed happily between the bobbing, boy-shaped silhouettes of my two friends as we picked our way through the tufts and troughs of coarse common grass, laughing and jostling each other, looking forward to tea and television.

I looked back once over my shoulder. I could just

make out the solitary figure of Duncan, still standing at the edge of the Marl Pit, still flicking his stick against his over-sized wellingtons, gazing up at the last livid streaks of day in an angry black sky. I don't think Roger looked back even once.

By the time I arrived home from my Northampton trip, I was in an unusually foul mood. My wife is wise. She waited, and eventually, when I'd eaten and got my pipe going, she asked me what was wrong.

'It's about this Duncan Tapman character, isn't it?' she said.

'Well, yes,' I replied, 'you see, I've always rather resisted the idea that one should go grubbing about in the past hoping to find something that will help explain the present. Perhaps I don't think enough about things like that. . . .'

# The Final Boundary

IT WAS MOSTLY dreams now. Sleeping dreams, waking dreams, he drifted from one to the other knowing that time was short and there was no good reason for dredging up the physical energy needed to return to what he used to call the real world. Too old, too sick, too tired, and there were no sons, daughters or close friends to cluster round the hospital bed demanding that he notice them. Someone fed him, someone washed him, other things happened, but they didn't really happen to him. They happened to the worn-out body lying on the bed, the body that would soon be surplus to requirements. A jolly good thing too, in his opinion. It couldn't come soon enough. A couple more dreams and then he would step into a completely different kind of reality, and his friend would be there to smile, and take his hand, and show him the way. He looked forward to that. He wanted it more than anything now—he really did.

One shadow only. One small but stubborn sadness was lodged immovably in a corner of his mind, and he couldn't even quite identify it. Something to do with—not failing exactly—but not succeeding enough, or in the right way perhaps. It was, he thought vaguely, rather like when you haven't quite finished a biscuit or a sandwich, and you've forgotten where you put it down. Your mouth knows there was one more bite to come, and you feel disappointed. It was a bit like that, only more so—something to do with the tone or quality of his life, an anger not released, a love not expressed, a final word not said, an exhilaration not felt—something in his life. . . .

It hadn't been a bad life, actually. Not eventful, but by no means unpleasant, and running through it all like two beautiful singing silver wires, his twin loves—cricket and Jesus. He heard a dry, wheezing little laugh coming from his own chest as he mouthed the words: 'Cricket—Jesus.' Folks would think he was barmy putting those two words together like that. But they did belong side by side, because that was where his soul had been for most of his life. In that game and that person. More in one than the other? No, it wasn't like that. Souls weren't like that. Jesus wasn't like that. He'd have made a jolly good cricketer, Jesus would. Leg spinner probably. Dead fair, but really crafty. Curl the ball all round your legs until, say, the fifth ball of his second over, then you'd jump out and go for a bad pitched one and it would break the other way and you'd be bowled, or stumped maybe. Opening bat he'd have been. Starting steady and firm and ending up dancing down the pitch to slam the ball to the boundary over and over again. Captain of course—he'd have to be captain. Useful to have Jesus around at the tea interval too, if it looked as if the cucumber sandwiches weren't going to go round. Yes, he'd have made a fine cricketer. . . .

A lot of his dreams were about cricket now. Two sorts. Some about things he'd really done, matches he'd really played in, and others about things he wished he'd done, triumphs he knew he had never really been capable of. One or two bad memories.

School—that was one of the real memories, and especially that day he'd gone down to the second eleven nets by invitation for the first time, feeling shy and nervous and clumsy as he took off his striped school blazer and laid it with the others by the two long cricket bags. He recalled wishing that the new cricket trousers he'd been sent by his mother weren't quite so beautifully creased and shinily white. He'd noticed how Bovington, the second's wicket keeper, glanced at him for an instant and smiled very slightly to himself as he turned back to bowl at the man in the net. Then old Raddish, the sports master, the one they all called 'Salad', had tossed one of the worn practice balls over to him and said in a loud voice, 'Come on then, Crocker, send one down. Let's see what you're made of!' He'd flushed, and only just caught the ball. He wanted to tell everyone that he was a batsman and not a bowler, but that wasn't the sort of thing you said in the nets. Everyone had a bowl in the nets, whatever they were best or worst at. His muscles had felt stiff and unco-ordinated as he stepped up to the single stump to send a slow one down to Evert-Brown, who was hitting everything with his usual elegant competence. And the worst had happened, the bally, blush-making worst! He'd let go of the ball before he should have done, sending it soaring up into the air and right over the top of the net, causing Evert-Brown to shield his eyes with his hand and gaze at the arcing sphere in mock astonishment as though it was a shooting star.

'Is it counted as a wide if it goes into orbit, Mr Raddish?' Bovington had called delightedly. 'Watch you don't burn your hands when you pick it up, Crocker. It'll be red hot after re-entry, you know.'

Bovington had been quickly extinguished by Salad, who was a lot kinder than he was wise, but the burning cheeks seemed to go on for ever, their heat matched only by his determination not to make a fool of himself when it came to the batting. And he hadn't made a fool of himself—not in the slightest. It had been a magical, utterly satisfying fifteen minutes. Whether the delivery was slow or fast, simple or tricky, the ball invariably arrived like a firm, friendly, rosy fruit, quivering and revolving in its eagerness to be struck with sweet and sensual rightness by the very centre of his bat. After only a few minutes with the pads on, he'd heard Evert-Brown say, 'He's got all the shots, sir.' And Salad had replied, 'Whacks 'em too, eh?' Even Bovington was impressed. He wandered round to the side of the net and stood watching for a minute or two, hands in his pockets, head on one side.

'Where'd you get your coaching?' he'd asked in the pause when the balls had to be collected from the sides of the net and sent back to the bowler's end.

He'd thought with a special, warm pleasure about the patient persistence of the quiet man at home.

'My dad. He taught me. We had a net in the garden.'

'Did a good job,' said Bovington. 'You're a fine bat.'

Heaven! One sort of heaven anyway, but, oddly enough, he'd never quite managed to get back into that particular kind of heaven again. Except, of course, in those other pretending dreams. He'd done amazing things in those. Double centuries against the Australians at Lords, match-winning boundaries against the West Indies, great performances that received tumultuous applause from thousands of admiring spectators. But in real life, although he became a fixture in the second eleven, and later in the first team, he'd never quite achieved the abandonment of that knock he'd enjoyed so much on his first visit to the second eleven net. It was the same in the local team he had joined after leaving school. He was nearly always good for double figures at least, and he frequently scored twenty or more. A few times he'd even reached the half century. Heaven within heaven! But it had only been a few times. Most of the time he had been a solid, reliable, unexciting batsman, contributing usefully and popular with the rest of the team, except for—*that* match. How well he remembered that nightmare of a match when they played away against a team called the Bottlers, who had a picturesque little pitch just over the county border in Kent. It must have been the first fixture they'd had with them. By golly, that match had been a nightmare too! He stirred uneasily in his bed at the memory.

Chap called Kendall was captain at the time. Rory Kendall. Nice chap, and a good captain. He'd won the toss and put the home side in to bat. It was a good toss to win, and there was no doubt that Kendall had made the right decision. There were huge grey clouds lumping around overhead, but they were on the move. By the time the Bottlers' last wicket went down for just over the hundred, the sun was out, and everything was set for the visitors to make the runs and claim the victory. Things didn't quite go according to plan though. The first three men, including Kendall who was a really skilful player, were all out before the score reached double figures. Kendall was run out after responding to a lunatic call from the other end, the lunatic was caught fairly miraculously when a full-blooded drive was held inches above the ground by a man fielding close to the bat, and the other was clean bowled by a ball that rose and straightened in an almost unplayable way. He remembered the captain's words in front of the pavilion as the third wicket went down: 'Take your time, Crocks old man. There's nothing out there to worry you too much. Hundred and three to win. We'll do it.'

The other thing he recalled was how he'd thought tentatively as he walked out to join Danny Whatsisname in the centre, that this could be it. This could just be his chance to do something sensational, something mildly—well—heroic. If he could stick there long enough to get some runs together, then a little flourish at the end—a bit of a hit! And at first it had looked as though that was exactly how it was going to work out. He played, very, very carefully until he was ready to open up a little, scoring in singles with the occasional two. The bowling presented no great problems. It was all pretty orthodox stuff. Nothing faster than slow-medium pace and the ball wasn't doing very much. The only thing that disturbed him was the way in which he was running out of partners at the other end. A combination of bad luck and carelessness sent one after another tramping dolefully or angrily back to the pavilion, leaving him to play with increased caution for fear that his wicket would go down as well, and that then the rot really would set in with a vengeance.

One fellow scored well. Walter Barnett. Not renowned for any technical skill with the bat, but nevertheless very strong, and very effective if he stayed long enough to get his eye in. He certainly got his eye in this time. Twenty off one over, twelve off another, and eight off a third, all scored in sixes and fours, dispatched with little elegance but enormous power to the rather short boundaries at the edge of the little rural ground. That was a great little innings, but nobody else matched it. By the time the ninth wicket went down, Crocker had scored twenty-nine runs, and the next highest score, by the number five, Percy Vidler, was eleven (apart from Walter's thirty of course). If the home team kept their over-rate up, there would be two overs of play remaining and ten runs needed for a win. The number eleven batsman was a tall, thin, fair-haired lad called Watkins, clearly petrified by the position he found himself in, and quite useless with a bat when he was relaxed, let alone now when the tension of the moment was causing him to twitch visibly. Still, it should be all right as long as Watkins could be kept at the non-strikers' end.

'Hang on to the bowling, Crocks. It's up to you now.'

That's what Kendall had shouted from the pavilion. Up to him! He could still feel the pungent mixture of excitement and fear that had gripped his stomach as the first ball of the over before last pitched at driving length in front of him, and he was able to lean forwards and stroke it smoothly back past the bowler for an easy two runs. Another two off the fourth ball, and from the sixth, a neat little steer through the slips which could have been another two if the single hadn't been needed for obvious strategic reasons. It was a good feeling. The runs were coming and *he* was getting them.

So there he'd been, A.J. Crocker, poised to accomplish what he'd dreamed of accomplishing so many times. Five runs to get from six balls against reasonably easy bowling, and he'd have won the match for his team, earned the applause of his friends, and deserved the congratulations of his captain. No Edwardian writer of public-school stories could have dreamed up a more dramatic scenario. 'Crocker of the lower fifth' was about to snatch victory from the jaws of whatever it was they always snatched it from in the books, for the sake of the jolly old school, and his chums in the lower fifth, and the head, who was a dashed good sort. What a lot of nonsense, but it honestly had felt a bit like that. Marvellous! The soft green grass of the out-field, the weighted plummy redness of the ball, the cool uniformed whiteness of the players, the wooden solidity of the bat in his hand, a sky that was now blue and clear of cloud, the merest hint of a breeze, and the opportunity to shine. What more could he ever ask for on this earth? As the bowler turned to begin his run for the first ball of the final over, he heard Kendall call out again!

'Let it go, Crocks! Let it go!'

Yes, that was exactly what he'd needed to do. Let it go! Only five runs. No problem. . . .

He didn't add a single run to the score in that last over. His toes curled even now as it came back to him, ball by ball. A great gloomy shadow of caution and fear had seemed to settle over him like a blanket as the first delivery looped its obvious way towards him. It was a gift of a ball—more like a beach ball than a cricket ball, made for crashing away to leg for four runs. That would have left only one run to get. He played a meticulous forward defensive stroke, killing the ball dead in front of his bat. Absolutely safe. Absolutely useless. Everything that should have been firm in him had turned to water. It was as though he was being reminded in the very centre of his will that permission to hit out and succeed had been withdrawn a long time ago. The second ball had been dead straight and a good length. He played defensively again. This time it was justified, but he knew that he'd have played the same shot if the ball had been suspended motionless in front of his bat with a little label attached to it saying 'hit me'. The third ball was like the first. This time he simply took a small step forwards, raised his bat, and let it pass quietly by outside the leg stump. Quaveringly sensitive, his ears detected a barely audible groan coming from the direction of the spectators grouped in front of the pavilion. 'Crocker of the lower fifth' was letting his chums down. Rory Kendall's voice, tense with frustration, had rung out across the ground once more.

'For goodness' sake *hit* it, Crocker!'

But he couldn't hit it. He couldn't let go. He couldn't find permission to drive his intention down from his eyes, through his body, through his arm, through his bat, through the ball, to the boundary and beyond. All the different parts of him withdrew from co-operative effort, so that the only automatic action left in him was the one he practised most. He blocked and blocked and blocked, and the game was lost.

Oh, the silence on his return to the others, the general air of puzzled dejection, the way in which Kendall had just shaken his head slowly from side to side as if unable to grasp the fact that something which had seemed to be already won could have been handed back with such scant resistance.

It was soon all right of course. They were a good crowd of chaps and, after all, he had scored thirty-four runs when all was said and done. He'd tried to explain to Kendall later on how he'd felt during that last over, but although Rory said it was all right, and not to worry about it, and it might happen to anyone, it was obvious that the captain was far too healthily straightforward and uncomplicated to understand what had really happened. Yes, it had been all right in the end, but he never quite had that kind of chance again. It was a shame he hadn't done better. A real shame.

Funny how those two memories were the ones that came back most now. That great knock in the nets as a lad, and much later, his failure against the Bottlers. Not that that failure had coloured all his cricketing memories. Goodness gracious, no! On the contrary. He'd always loved being one of a crowd of fellows; really enjoyed belonging. The warm familiarness of home matches, the bustle of travel to away fixtures, the matches themselves, offering the ever-new opportunity to do well, if not brilliantly, and the time in the pub afterwards drinking just a little too much as the big enamel jug full of frothing draught bitter was passed round the increasingly mellow company. It had all been grand. Grand times, grand chaps, a grand game. . . .

And Jesus? Well, now that he thought about it, his friendship with Jesus had become more and more private as the years went by, more and more something that turned into a badly wrapped parcel as soon as you tried to tie it up with words. Maybe that was wrong, but it was a fact.

It hadn't always been like that, of course. He'd first met Jesus in a church where everybody talked about it all the time. He'd been the same. It was so exciting, so explosively invigorating to discover a love that had been directed to him personally since before the beginning of time, so thrilling to feel that he'd hit on the truth that underpinned the whole of creation—of existence. He'd felt a burning need to pass on to others the shining wonder of his encounter with the living God. Everywhere he went, his Bible went with him. Everyone he spoke to was likely to hear something about his faith, even in the course of very brief conversations. People in cafés, on trains, standing at bus-stops, at work or on holiday, they all got a little evangelical blast.

That wheezing chuckle rocked his slight frame once more. All those poor people having to put up with that young religious fanatic with the big black Bible and the shiny eyes. Anyone who had seen him coming the second time round must have given him a very wide berth indeed. He'd been far too pushy and crude. He knew that now. And yet—there was a strange sweet sadness in the memory of those days, something about the freshness and naïvety of his attitude to the whole business of expressing his faith, that he wished he could have hung on to a bit more as the years went by. Not that he'd altogether stopped telling people what he believed. He'd never actually done that, but he had learned not to shove it down people's throats. He'd come to realize that everyone needs space and respect and gentleness, and that only God ever did any real changing in anyone's life. Nevertheless, he knew deep inside himself that he'd never taken the trouble, or found the courage, to develop a language and an approach that would really convey the depth and importance of the love he felt for Jesus. Not in ordinary situations—not naturally.

Jesus. Strange really how, for him, Jesus had become something separate from religion and church and formulas and that sort of thing. And the reason for that, he was sure, was that when all those things had become meaningless to him for a while, Jesus had still been around, a stubborn friend who let abuse and rejection ride right over him when the dark times came—and there had been very dark times once or twice. What was it they quoted Karl

Marx as saying: 'I am not a Marxist.'

If Jesus came back today, would he be tempted to say, 'I am not a Christian.' Was that an irreverent thought? He didn't know. Didn't care much either. It certainly didn't matter any more what any other human being on earth felt about what he thought or didn't think, believed or didn't believe. All that was left for him out of the world's great religious jumble sale was Jesus, living now, with him and waiting for him, sometimes on the cross and sometimes off it, depending on whether he was being made to suffer or not. And it wouldn't be long now before he met him in a completely new way and all the things that hadn't made sense before would be explained. All would be well. He was ready. Well—almost ready.

Why had he never talked to his cricketing friends about Jesus? What was it that had stopped him from openly mixing the two most important things in his life? Because he hadn't mixed them at all, in all the time that he'd played. A little over thirty years as a member of the team, and another twenty as a non-playing associate of the club. Naturally, he'd always done his best to be helpful and generous and all the other things that were important, but that wasn't the whole point, and he knew it. Why had he never shared the other great passion of his life with people he met once or twice a week—every week in the summer—for years and years and years?

Perhaps he'd believed that his total enjoyment of cricket was actually very fragile. Was it that he feared an alienation, a separation from the ordinariness of the activity that he relished? Had it, in fact, been a worry that he wouldn't be able to belong to it a hundred per cent any more if he once revealed that something else and unearthly burned in him?

What a lot of nonsense he was thinking! Did it really matter? No point in getting all worked up and troubled about it now. Better to just go on dreaming and wait quietly for the end. Even if he hadn't got it dead right, even if he had fallen short in one or two areas, it was too late to do anything about it now, and he knew he'd be forgiven for all the rotten things he'd done, and the caring things he hadn't. You could trust God for that as long as you had Jesus beside you. It was just that . . . well, it was a pity he couldn't have rooted out that little shadow before he went. Rooted it out, seen what it was, and got rid of it. He sighed a little as he felt his body and mind slipping from consciousness to sleep.

He dreamed about Kendall that night. Kendall, long dead in reality, but young and straight and fit in the dream, just as he'd looked forty years ago. There was no question that it was him, despite the fact that he seemed to be a very long way away. His hands were cupped around his mouth, and he was shouting something. No matter how much effort he put into these shouts, though, it just wasn't possible to make out what he was saying because there was another and much greater noise that completely drowned out his voice. On investigation the sound turned out to be the roar of a deep and swiftly flowing river, dangerously split and thrown up into spray by angry black rocks. Kendall was standing on the far bank of the river, legs apart, head up, calling and calling for all he was worth. It wasn't quite the same as the way he had called out from the pavilion on the day of the Bottlers match—much more intense, more urgent. He was asking—pleading— for Crocker to do something for him. Then, the noise of the river must have decreased, or Kendall must have started to shout even more loudly, because one or two words began to filter through to the listener's ears: 'Please, Crocks . . . over here . . . please!'

There was no mistaking Kendall's message now. He was asking him to come across that dreadful river for some reason. Well, imploring rather than asking. Fearfully he peered down into the racing, leaping, tumultuous grey waters and felt the same paralysis of mind and body that had allowed the opposing team to achieve an effortless win on that pretty little cricket ground all those years ago. He knew that nothing would make him jump down into that terrible current.

Standing limply on his bank of the river, he looked up again and saw that Rory Kendall had given up shouting. He was just standing quietly now, hands in his pockets, gazing up at the sky as if waiting for something. He couldn't have been heard any more in any case. The noise of the rushing waters had suddenly become deafening. Strangely, too, it was becoming more and more difficult even to see the slim figure in the distance because, although on this side of the river the sun was shining and the air was bright, over where Kendall was, night was falling.

For once it was a relief to wake up, to be able to remind himself that it had just been a dream—that there was no fast-flowing river, that Kendall had passed on a long time ago, and that he hadn't really failed him again, except in a meaningless nightmare. But his peace was gone. Unaccountably, the little shadow had grown like a cancer and was darkening his spirit at a time when he should simply have been looking forward to meeting Jesus. Jesus? Where was Jesus? For the first time for a long time he had no sense of his friend being present. Dimly he became aware that someone was wiping his eyes and his cheeks. Far away in the distance he heard a woman speak: 'Poor old chap. He's been crying in his sleep. Won't be long now.'

He tried hard to make the right kind of waking dreams come; he'd been able to do that quite easily up to now, but he didn't seem to have the same kind of control any more. Memories, pleasant and unpleasant, ran into each other like spilled colours, swirling confusedly around his tired brain, preventing him from following a broad and peaceful pathway to death. But underneath all the confusion, from a small clear space in his mind, a voice—his voice—spoke the same prayer again and again with passionate urgency: 'One more chance! Please give me one more chance. . . .' And then—the confusion stopped abruptly, and the last dream of all came.

It was one of those dreams where colours and sounds and smells were vivid and real, as though he was wide awake, but in the wrong place. He found himself standing at the edge of the most beautifully serene lake, broad and still, surrounded on three sides by thick, lush woodland, while in the distance, heavily elegant hills stepped gently up into mountainhood. The air was still and sweet beneath a sky of subtle, water-colour blue. Birds were singing. A slight breeze moved his hair. It was perfect cricketing weather, and looking down he realized that, appropriately enough, he was dressed not only in white shirt, trousers and boots, but also in a pair of batting pads. Nor was that all, for lying beside his feet on the bank was something that looked very much like a favourite old bat of his, the one that had split during a match played on his fortieth birthday, much to the amusement of his team mates. He picked it up and stroked the yellow wood gently with the tips of his fingers. There was no doubt about it. It was his bat, miraculously restored, as good as ever, well oiled and ready for action. It was like meeting an old friend. His own body seemed to be pretty well restored as well. Not, perhaps, to the first flush of youth, but certainly to the sort of lazy fitness he'd enjoyed in his late thirties.

He swung the bat briskly through the air a couple of times. Presumably all this gear meant there was a match on. Great stuff! But where was the pitch? Turning round and away from the water he saw, directly in front of him, a perfectly shaped, dead-flat rectangle of closely mown grass, like a little lawn in the midst of the undergrowth. Set in the centre of this ten-yard-by-five-yard area was a set of cricket stumps, complete with a pair of bails; and newly painted on the grass in front of the wicket, on the side furthest from the lake, were the white lines that marked the batting and 'popping' creases. A strange sort of cricket pitch with only one set of stumps, no fielders, no bowler and no umpires, but in his dream it all seemed quite natural. This was where he was to bat. He would simply take guard and wait. Someone would bowl to him eventually. Yes, it all seemed quite natural, and how wonderful to have the chance of a final knock.

As he took up his position at the crease, flexing his shoulders and patting the ground with the end of his bat in the old familiar way, he wondered what kind of attack he would be facing. Looking up, he could see nothing but low thick undergrowth stretching away into the distance, with the odd tree dotted here and there. Then, far, far away in the pale blue sky above the horizon, a tiny speck appeared, so small that it was hardly visible. Shading his eyes with his left hand, he stared intently at the distant object. It was very gradually increasing in size. Although still minute, the thing, whatever it was, was travelling in his direction at tremendous speed, and he knew with absolute certainty, as one does in dreams, that this was the ordained target for his bat. This was the thing he was supposed to hit, and it was coming closer by the second.

'Hit out, Crocker! Give it all you've got!'

The voice came from his left. Snatching a glance in that direction, he saw that its owner was sitting on a grassy slope, his posture that of a typical cricket watcher—one leg outstretched, the other bent, and the top half of his body leaning its weight back on elbows and forearms, the very picture of keen relaxation. He had never seen the man before, but he knew who it was.

Switching his attention back to the task in hand, he found that the approaching target had acquired shape and colour. Whatever else it might be, it certainly was not a cricket ball. The shape was too shiftingly irregular for that and the colours were not right—blue, red and white, with a suggestion of yellow as well. It looked like nothing so much as a brightly coloured scarf or a wide ribbon curled loosely into the rough shape of a ball, forming and twisting and reforming as it hurtled towards him. It was also much, much bigger than a cricket ball. The speed and distance had been deceptive.

It was a snake—a huge, serpent-like creature with an evil flattened head, a tapering, pointed tail, and a horrible fleshy weightiness about the centre part of its body. It was close enough now for him to be able to see two little eyes glinting from a head that stayed quite still as the rest of the body rolled and coiled through the air. In seconds it would be upon him, heavy, vicious, enveloping, and able to be defeated only by one sound blow with the incongruously slight length of willow that at present rested quietly in his gloved hands. It was the chance he'd prayed for. Just one good hit. . . .

'Let go, Crocks! Let it go!'

Dread seized him as the voice rang out once more. He was going to fail again. Cold fear drained down through his body seeming to deepen his shadow on the close-cropped grass. It was going to happen all over again. He would make some feeble defensive gesture, there would be groans of disappointment, and the game, or battle, or victory, would be lost—irretrievably lost.

'Do it for *me*, Crocker!'

A strange illusion—that the words came arcing through the air, to enter, not through his ears, but straight into his chest, into his heart, warming and strengthening every part of him in a way he had never experienced before. Not before time either. With a furious hissing noise and an unspeakably nauseating stench, the creature filled his vision and was within hitting range. With a little stab of pure joy he raised his bat and dealt a thunderously perfect blow straight to the underside of the malevolently thrusting head. The follow-through was flawless. Despite its great weight, the serpent's body seemed to fly from the bat, sailing through the air in the direction from which it had come, its mouth emitting a loud scream of frustration which faded and died as the flailing blue and red carcass disappeared into the distance.

Filled with a thrilling ecstasy he dropped his bat and filled his lungs with sweet, clean air. A narrow path led away through the undergrowth to his left. He followed it to where it opened out onto the hillside, then stopped and looked up. The man was on his feet now, and even from a distance it was obvious that he was smiling. He took a step forwards and held out his hand. . . .

'Mr Crocker's gone.'

'Poor old chap. Best really, eh?'

'Yes, you're right. Went happy though. Look at that smile , . . .'

# The Visit

## – 1 –

OUR CHURCH USED to be very okay. We did
all the things that churches do just about as well as
they could be done, and we talked about our founder with reverence and proper gratitude. We said
how much we would have liked to meet him when
he was around and how much we looked forward to
seeing him at some remote time in the future.

The unexpected news that he was going to pay us
an extended visit now, in the present, was, to say the
least, very disturbing. All confident statements
about 'the faith' tended to dry up. People who had
always seemed reasonably cheerful looked rather
worried. Those who had been troubled appeared to
brighten considerably.

A man who had always said that 'atonement was a
peculiarly Jewish idea' became extremely thoughtful. Someone who had published a pamphlet
entitled 'The Real Meaning of the Resurrection

Myth' joined the mid-week prayer group and developed an open mind. Desperate folk just counted the days.

Each of us, I suppose, reacted to the news in our own way, but I think the thing we had in common was a feeling that the game (albeit a very sincere and meaningful game for some) was over. No more pretending when he came. He would know.

As for myself, I was looking forward to him coming, as long as it worked out 'all right'—if you see what I mean. I was an organizer, a doer. My job was to keep the life of the church community tidy, make sure that the right people ended up in the right place doing the right things, and I enjoyed being good at it. Granted, I wasn't one of the super-spiritual types, but I smiled and sang with the rest on a Sunday and I seemed to be liked and respected by most folk. God? Well, I suppose my relationship with God was a bit like a marriage without sex—if I'm honest. I'd never got close. But—I worked hard, and I felt I must have earned a small bed-sit in heaven, if not a mansion.

So, my job was to organize our founder's visit, make sure it went smoothly, and generally master-mind the whole event. Before long I'd prepared a programme for the day of his arrival and even sorted out who he'd stay with. There was a little wrangling about who that should be. Somebody said that it should be a person who was the same at home as they were at church, and someone else said that in that case he'd have to stay in a hotel, but in the end I just chose who it would be and that was that.

My main problem was that I wasn't able to contact him in advance to talk about the arrangements. All I actually knew was that he would arrive for evening service on Sunday, but I wasn't worried. In my experience, visitors were only too pleased to slot into a clear order of events and I assumed that he, of all people, wouldn't want to rock somebody else's carefully balanced boat. Isn't it odd when you look back and remember thinking ridiculous thoughts like that? At the time it seemed quite reasonable and I was so used to tying up loose ends (even when there weren't any to tie sometimes), that it never occurred to me that somebody who embodied the very essence and spirit of creativity might, as it were, bring his own loose ends with him.

As the day of the visit drew closer, a sort of mild panic passed through the church. One person said that she felt a visit 'in the flesh' lacked taste and was likely to corrupt the purity of her vision of God, another that in his view it was taking things 'too far'. One man, hitherto regarded as being a most saintly character, confessed to an array of quite startling sins thus becoming, in the eyes of the church, less admirable but far more interesting and approachable. One sweet old lady cornered me one evening in the church room and anxiously asked me the question which probably troubled most of us: 'Is it true that he knows . . . everything we think?'

I didn't know the answers to questions like that. I just wanted things to go well and looked forward, as I usually did, to the time when it was all over and we could look back and say, 'It really went well,' and, 'Wasn't it worth while?' I'm afraid it was to be some time before I learned not to stash experiences safely away in the past before they had a chance to change me.

Anyway, Sunday arrived at last and sure enough—he came.

Now, I know it seems an awful thing to say, but at first it looked as if it was going to be a terrible disappointment—an anticlimax. He wasn't quite what we'd expected. He was rather too . . . real. His arrival was odd too. I'd planned it to be quite an occasion, and maybe I was wrong but I was hoping for something in the way of a grand entrance.

Everything was set up, everyone in their places, when we suddenly realized that the man we were waiting for was already there, sitting quietly in the back row. To be honest, I wouldn't have recognized him but, thank goodness, somebody did and suggested he came out to the front.

Well, I was just thinking, 'Great, we can get started now,' but I hadn't even spoken to him when he turned to face the congregation and said (and you're not going to believe this), 'Has anyone got a sandwich?' Well, a few people laughed, but one old lady went straight round the back to the kitchen and made him a sandwich and a cup of tea, and when she brought them back he sat down on the steps and enjoyed them without any sign of self-consciousness.

I was completely thrown by this. I'd got a copy of the programme in my hand, but when I pulled myself together enough to move towards him, he stood up, turned round and looked at me, and I just couldn't give it to him. I can't describe the look he gave me. It made me want to cry and hit him. That sounds ridiculous, doesn't it, but he made me feel like an idiot, and I admit that I felt oddly ashamed as well. But why?

Anyway, he turned to face all the people again and he looked at them as if he was looking for a friend in a crowd. He seemed to be searching for a face he knew. Then someone waved to him and this is where the whole thing just got silly. He ran down the aisle and put his arms round this woman in the fourth row, and she was crying, and he was saying something to her that none of us could hear, and then some other people got up and went over to him until there was quite a little crowd with him in the middle of it.

It was weird. You see, there were people still sitting in their seats, still facing the front, obviously embarrassed and not knowing what to do, while over at the side was this knot of people laughing and crying and making one heck of a noise. Then . . . all the noise stopped. Quite suddenly, when he put his hand up, there was absolute silence.

Over at the other side of the church a young fellow was sitting, facing the front, and he seemed to be paralysed. His face was white, his hands were clenched on his knees, and he seemed to be holding himself together by an effort of will. Then there were these two words that seemed to unlock him somehow.

'Don't worry.' That was all. Just, 'Don't worry,' and that young fellow went flying across the church and skidded to a halt on his knees. And then it started all over again—the noise I mean—and then they all went out. They just . . . went out.

I followed them to the door and I actually managed to catch hold of his coat sleeve.

'Excuse me,' I said, 'I thought we were all going to be together for the service.'

'Of course,' he said and smiled, 'please come with us.'

I just didn't know what to do then.

'But we usually have the service in church.'

'Wouldn't you rather come with me?' he said.

Well, I would have really, but I didn't know where he was going to go. I thought he was going to fit in with us, and he seemed so . . . haphazard.

'Where *are* you going?' I asked.

He looked up and down the street (and here's another thing you won't believe), pointed across the street and said, 'What's that pub like?'

I said, 'It's a bit rough really,' and anyway, I knew

for a fact that two or three of the people with him wouldn't go into a pub on principle. At least I thought I knew, because they all trailed in there after him; young fellows, maiden aunts, old men—the lot. I was stunned.

I stood by the church door for half an hour and round about half past seven he came out again, and I swear to you he had more people with him when he came out than when he went in. They all swarmed back over the road to the church and he said to me, 'Can we come back in now?'

So they all came back in and sat down. Well, I say sat down—they hung themselves on the backs of pews, sat cross-legged on the floor, draped themselves over the radiators, just anyhow, and he started to talk to them. (All the people who had stayed in the church had gone by then, including the lady he was supposed to be staying with.)

Now, this is the bit I don't understand. He'd spoiled my service, everything had gone wrong, and he'd made me feel really stupid, but more than anything I wanted to sit down on the floor and listen to him talk—and I got the feeling that he wanted me to.

But I didn't.

I went home.

You know, I haven't cried, not really cried, since I was a little boy, but that night I sat at home and cried my eyes out. Then quite suddenly I knew what to do. I slammed out of the house and ran back to the church. It was so quiet when I got there, I thought they must have all gone, but when I went in there was just him sitting there. He smiled warmly.

'You took your time,' he said, 'I've been waiting for you. I'm staying at your house tonight.'

# – 2 –

ON THE DAY that our founder caused such an uproar by returning to the church in person, I nearly lost the chance to be with him, largely because I couldn't accept his refusal to fit in with what I wanted. That got sorted out, and he actually came to live in my house for a time before we found somewhere more suitable.

You'd think I'd learned my lesson, wouldn't you? I hadn't.

I lived with him, worked with him, saw him do some amazing things, grew to love him even, but I became increasingly infuriated by the way he was distracted by trivial things—or what I saw as trivial things. I still hadn't learned that everything he did always had a reason. Always.

As a result of the anger building up in me, I lost him once again, and this time it was nearly for good.

It happened a few months after his arrival, before he became really well known, and it happened in London. He'd never been there before, but now he'd been asked to speak to a group in the city, so he went, and I went with him. He wasn't always very practical about things like money and tickets and time. My job was simply to make sure he got where he was supposed to be.

We had to go from Kings Cross to Victoria on the tube at the end of our journey, and that was difficult enough. I was tired, the train was packed, and when we finally arrived he kept stopping on the platform and staring at people as they crushed around and past him. Each time I managed to sort of tilt him into motion again, but when we neared the foot of the escalator he stopped again, and stood like a rock in the rapids, refusing to budge.

We were late already, and I could feel my patience

fading as the knot of anger that seemed to be there all the time nowadays was tightened just a little more. Even so, I'd learned enough about him by then to know that there was simply no shifting him once he'd got a bee in his bonnet, not until he'd done something about it—the right thing. You could always tell when he thought he had done 'the right thing'. His face would relax and he'd smile like a happy child.

When I asked him what was up, he pointed towards the tiled side wall where an old man with one arm was playing a harmonica incredibly badly, and with no great success judging by the pathetic little handful of copper coins lying in the hat by his feet.

He looked at the old man for a moment, then turned to me with a rather desperate look and said, 'What are we supposed to do?'

'Put some money in the hat,' I said, 'if you want to. But whether you do or you don't, hurry please, we must get on!'

He patted the pockets of his jacket. It was a very smart jacket. I'd managed to persuade him to buy one really smart thing to wear for occasions like the one we were heading for.

'I haven't any money,' he said. 'Have you?'

We edged over to the man and dropped something in his cap. At the sight of a note among his little collection of coppers, the old fellow nearly swallowed his mouth organ. Then we let the crowd sweep us forward and soon we were safely wedged on the escalator.

I turned amid the din of the machinery, and the people's voices, and the fading wail of the harmonica, and looked into his face—to check, I suppose. My heart sank. No relaxed smile. His eyes were full of concern and distraction, and I probably knew what he was going to do even before he did it.

Suddenly, he was gone, burrowing his way back down the escalator until I lost sight of him. As he went I just caught the words: 'I'll see you at the top.'

When I reached the top I was fuming. It was getting really late now, and this was an important meeting we were going to, and he was screwing it up!

I leaned on a ticket machine and waited.

After what seemed like an age, his face slowly emerged over the top of the escalator, beaming satisfaction—and that was okay—but when the rest of him appeared I just felt cold fury. He was wearing a crudely patterned jacket that was ludicrously small for him, and even more absurd, one of the sleeves had been cut off at the armhole and sewn together at the shoulder.

I don't think I even spoke to him, I was so angry. I just marched off and assumed that he wouldn't dare do anything else to hold us up. By the time we got to the hall where he was due to speak I'm afraid I wasn't in very good shape. Don't forget, I didn't understand him as well then as I did later, and it mattered to me terribly what people thought of him—of us—well, all right—me.

I feel terrible when I think of how I felt then, and what I did. As we started to mount the steps towards the big double doors at the top, I looked at this absurd figure who claimed so much but sometimes seemed to behave like a weak, stupid person, and to put it bluntly—I was ashamed of him. I deliberately hung back at the bottom of the steps and watched as a little knot of anxious-looking men drew him in. Even from where I was I could see they were looking at him askance in his ridiculous music-hall coat.

The next moment burned itself into my memory.

He turned round and looked at me, not with anger or annoyance, but with bewilderment and need. He needed his friend with him in those strange surroundings. But by then I'd drawn back, out of sight, into the darkness, and I wasn't there.

It was then that I lost him—not on the escalator. I didn't wait for him to come out that night, and to this day I don't know how the talk went, or how he got home without a ticket, or anything.

I didn't try to contact him again. I stopped going to the church, and I avoided places where we might have met. I spent the next few months trying to convince myself that I was better off without him, but I suppose—secretly—I knew that I'd lost the most important thing I'd ever had. It was the second time I'd walked out on him since we met, and I assumed he wouldn't be very interested in seeing me after I'd deserted him when he needed me most.

By the time I did meet him again, he'd become well known all over the country. He'd made a lot of friends and a few rather heavy enemies as well. What with the healings and the big meetings, he was always in the papers or on television, and every time I saw his face a huge grief welled up in me and I had to do something else—quickly. I'd cut myself off because of a stupid jacket and my own foolish pride. I cursed myself over and over again.

One summer morning, when work had taken me back to London, I went for a stroll in the park near my hotel, and there *he* was, sitting all alone on a bench beside the path. He was gazing at an unopened letter, held at arm's length as though it was about to explode. Everything in me except the small part that really matters, decided to turn back before he saw me. I didn't. I walked forward and sat down quietly but rigidly beside him, my whole body and mind clenched against rejection. The expression on his face when he turned his head was not one of surprise. It was a mixture of deep pleasure and relief, with not a trace of resentment. I was too near to tears to speak, but he handed me the letter and said, 'I'm afraid this may be bad news. Would you open it and tell me what it says please?' He turned his head and stared sightlessly over the park, while I opened the letter with rather shaky hands and read it aloud.

It was bad news. One of his closest friends, someone who had welcomed him and shared his vision from the beginning, had died quite suddenly after a massive heart attack.

As I finished reading the letter a strange thing happened. He closed his eyes, and sighed from somewhere deep inside him. Simultaneously a breeze moved across the grass and ruffled the leaves on the trees that lined the path. It was as if the natural world was gently sighing in sympathy with him.

Then the moment was past.

He turned back to me and said, 'I'm glad I had time for a little pain, and I'm glad you were here with me. Now. . . .'

'Now?' I said, 'What do you want me to do . . . now?'

'Do? I want you to do what you always did. I'm seeing people all the time—every day. I want you to organize me, bully me, help me to help them. You can even . . . choose my jackets for me if you like.'

I had to ask him. 'Look! Could you just tell me . . . on that day in the tube, why was it so important for you to go back and swap jackets? It seemed such a pointless gesture. I mean . . . what use was a jacket with two sleeves to a man with one arm?'

He looked at me steadily for a moment, then smiled shyly. 'None,' he said. 'Actually, I didn't go back to swap jackets, but in the end I felt I had to.'

'Had to?'

His smile broadened. 'You can't leave a man with a new arm and no sleeve to put it in, can you?'

He took the letter and envelope from my hand, stood up, and dropped them deliberately into a litter bin by the seat.

'Are you coming?' he asked, and he stepped out purposefully in the sunshine across the park.

Without a word I got up and followed him, towards the city.

## – 3 –

I WANTED TO SEE a miracle.

Just one.

One solid, absolutely indisputable, gold-plated miracle, happening before my very eyes.

A small one would do—that would be fine. One ordinary little miracle.

There were two main snags.

First, I didn't want to be the kind of person who needed to see a miracle. I wanted to have the kind of deep, impressive faith that would quietly acknowledge amazing healings, for instance, as mere confirmation of the things I already believed.

Secondly, I kept missing them. In the weeks since our founder had begun his visit to the church, it had soon become clear that he intended to do the same things in the eighties as he had done in the distant past, and this included miraculous healings. As usual, people's reactions varied from fascination to hostility, with a strong flavouring of fear. As he himself put it, what a lot of folk really wanted from him was an hour of Paul Daniels, two choruses of 'My Way', and a nice tidy exit through the skylight.

However, the visit continued, and so did the

healings.

There were no rules about time and place as far as I could see. It might be a child in the supermarket or an invalid at home or an old man in a pub. The only thing that these incidents had in common (from my point of view) was that I was never quite there to see them.

After the misunderstanding between us when he first arrived, I had begun to learn that the formulae and lists and structures were not as important as I thought. He said, though, that I should go on using my talent as an organizer to leave him free to work with people. So I did, and as a result I was busy most of the time, especially as I still had a full-time job as well in those days. It seemed to me that I'd always just left the church, or just turned the corner of the street, or just popped out of the pub for a moment, when something miraculous happened in the place where I'd just been. Later, someone would rush up to me excitedly and say, 'You're not going to believe what happened after you left this morning. It was quite incredible . . . ,' and so on.

It became more and more difficult to respond to news of this sort with the right kind of enthusiasm. It takes enormous effort to crinkle your eyes into a Christian smile and say, 'Gosh, how wonderful!' when you actually want to sneer and say, 'Oh yes, and you saw it, didn't you, and I didn't, did I?'

It wasn't, you understand, that I didn't believe in healings. It was just that . . . I didn't believe in them. It's hard to explain what I mean. I knew some of the people who were made better. I knew them before they were healed, and I knew them afterwards. Clearly, something amazing had happened and I was duly amazed, and more than ready to defend the truth of their experiences to anybody. It was just that some part of me, a child frightened of being conned by the grown-ups perhaps, wanted to actually *see*.

Now, you might say to me, 'Why didn't you just tell him how you felt? You could have asked him to give you a shout next time something was about to happen.' And I agree that sounds like a reasonable suggestion. The fact was, though, that he was no easier to predict or pin down now than he had been during his first visit all those years ago. I could never be quite sure how he'd react to questions or comments or people or events. Just as I thought I'd established what he would do in a particular situation, he'd do something quite different and even tell me off for saying something that I fondly imagined to be just the sort of supportive comment that he needed.

I remember once, he was sitting with someone in a small back room that we used for interviewing and counselling. I can't recall now who it was, but he or she had just gone through some awful experience and had asked to speak to him privately. I was sitting in the main body of the church, twiddling my thumbs and waiting for him, when a small group of young children clattered in through the front door and said they'd come to see 'the nice man'. Well, he always loved being with children, and I thought I knew him well enough to guess the right thing to do, so, all in good faith I told them to go through to the back and find him.

Good faith! Now I'll tell you what I really thought. Two things occurred to me, in the following order.

First, my common sense told me that the children should wait until he'd finished what was probably a very delicate and intimate conversation. Right on top of that perfectly reasonable thought came the memory of another occasion when children had wanted to see him and his friends had prevented them. I reached over for a Bible from the pile beside me and leafed through the pages to check the reference. Yes, there it was in black and white. Matthew, chapter nineteen, verse fourteen: 'Let the little children come to me, and do not hinder them.' A different setting, but the same principle, surely? I wasn't going to get it wrong the way those chaps had. Perhaps I would even earn a word of praise for my thoughtfulness.

Wrong again. He was not pleased. The children reappeared almost immediately. They seemed quite happy, but when he finally joined me, he made it quite clear that, in his view, my first instinct had been the correct one.

My cheeks burn as I remember how at that moment, defensive and flustered, the Bible still open on my knees, I came very close to quoting Scripture to put him back on the straight and narrow. He knew what I was thinking. He always did. He pointed. 'That book,' he said, 'is like the sabbath. It's made for you, not the other way round.'

It was a point that he made again and again to various people in various ways. He never ceased to be amazed and saddened by the way people seemed to prefer rules and laws and set ways of doing things, to what he once called the 'organized madness of love'. The problem for me was that organized madness could mean doing the sensible thing, or it could mean stepping out and walking on the water. I kept getting it wrong, and that's why I wasn't keen to bring up the subject of miracles. I had an uneasy feeling that he would see straight through my question and produce a question of his own. Something like: 'Who do you think that I am?' The strictly honest answer to that question would be, 'I'll tell you when I've seen a miracle.' In other words, I suspected that the root of my problem might be plain old-fashioned doubt.

The whole thing came to a head when my elderly mother was sent home from hospital after exploratory surgery revealed that she had inoperable cancer. She was given a month to live, and she only had me to spend that month with, so I installed her in a downstairs room and arranged time off work to be with her.

My relationship with my mother had always been an area of pain and guilt for me. As far as I could gather, she had put on disappointment and pessimism like a coat when she was a small child, and she seemed determined to wear that coat to her death. Her only warm memory, or the only one she ever mentioned to me, was of her father, who died when she was seven. She told me in a rare moment of intimacy that only the memory of his eyes shining with love carried her through the years after his death. She was rejected by her mother, and later made a disastrous early marriage to my father who bullied and neglected both of us until his death some years ago. She seemed to have made a decision early in her life that it was dangerous to be vulnerable and therefore she would never be vulnerable again. As a result of this I grew up surrounded by negatives and believing, as children can easily do, that I had failed in the task of giving my mother the love that she never got from anyone else.

I remember walking into the kitchen after school one day and finding my mother peeling potatoes at the sink. Something about the stubborn misery with which she was performing that ordinary task ripped into me at that moment and, for once, my feelings spilled over into words. Tears of anger and self-pity broke up the image of her resigned figure as I shouted through clenched teeth: 'I'm sorry . . . I'm sorry, Mum. It's not my fault . . . it's not . . . it's not.

I'm here too. . . .'

It was the only occasion that I can remember her touching me. My vision was still blurred but I felt the pressure of her hand on my shoulder, and, strange as it may seem, that moment of communication, wordless though it was, allowed me to forgive a lot of the discouragement and apparent lack of affection that I suffered in the following years.

And now she was going to die.

As I sat by her bed and studied the grey face, marked with lines of disillusionment and tense with physical pain, I wondered why he hadn't come. I had telephoned places where he might be, places where he had just been, places where he was due to arrive. I had left messages everywhere asking him to come to my house as soon as he could, and still he hadn't come. The thing that hurt me was that he knew anyway. He must know. He knew everything. At any rate, if he was who he said he was, he knew everything.

Realizing that she had passed into real sleep at last, I made my way wearily through to the kitchen to make yet another mug of strong coffee. My head ached with fatigue and worry as I spooned coffee and sugar into the mug and poured hot water from the kettle. It was as I took my first sip of the hot, sweet liquid that I heard the sound of a man's voice coming from my mother's room. My tired brain whirled helplessly. The doors—front and back— were locked. There was no way in. There was no way that anybody could have got in. No way. . . . Suddenly, calmly, I knew.

He had come.

I slowly pushed the bedroom door open and there he was, sitting on her bed holding one of her hands in both of his and saying something very softly to her. I sat down as quietly as I could on the other side of the bed. What was he going to do?

He glanced up at me briefly and smiled, then turned back to my mother. She was awake and gazing straight into his face, her eyes wider than I remembered. I stared, fascinated, and moved too deeply for words as her face softened and sweetened, the creases of despair and disappointment reforming into lines of laughter and happiness. And her eyes had become the eyes of a child, a child who knew beyond question that she was loved and wanted at last. Her lips moved, and as I leaned forwards, I heard her whisper, 'Father, father.'

Then she turned to me and looked at me in the way I had always wanted her to. I took the hand she was trying to lift to me and she just said two words: 'All right, son?' It was an apology, a question and a reassurance. It was all I needed.

Then she turned back to him and said, 'I'd like to see you again.'

'You will,' he said, 'soon.' Then she died, in a room full of peace.

Since then I have seen people made better quite dramatically, but nothing has touched or changed me more than those few minutes at my mother's bedside. I have never seen such love, never seen such healing.

I had seen a miracle.

– 4 –

I STARTED PACKING at midnight on Saturday. By force of habit I did it as carefully and precisely as I always did everything, but my thoughts were in tatters and I made little whimpering noises as I folded shirts and jumpers, and pushed shoes and slippers into the usual non-existent gaps. Around one o'clock I fastened the last strap on the last suitcase with hands that trembled slightly but uncontrollably, and stood it in the hall next to the others. It seemed crucially important that they should be exactly parallel, and for some minutes I made miniscule adjustments to each case until I was satisfied.

Pushing the hair back from my forehead with the flat of my hand, I studied the assembled luggage anxiously, hoping that there was something else I needed to do—anything to postpone the moment when guilt and fear would fill the vacuum in my mind yet again. There was nothing left to do though, and no hope of sleep. I turned off the hall light and slid down onto the carpet beside my suitcases. Nobody could reach me now. I had already taken the phone off the hook, its ringing had filled me with dread for days, and if anyone came to the door I just wouldn't open it. I wouldn't so much as move a muscle until dawn, then a taxi to the station, and that would be that.

I had hardly slept for more than a week, and tonight I knew that I couldn't stand it any more, I just couldn't stand it—the guilt, the despair, the futile attempts to distract myself, the endless cups of coffee in the early hours, and worst of all the flood of graphic scenes involving exposure and humiliation, pumped out remorselessly by my imagination.

There were only two ways I could go. One, meeting the problem head on, was unthinkable—I hadn't the courage. The other was simply to go, just leave and lose myself in the busyness of some other town or city where nobody knew or cared who I was or what I'd done. I just wanted some peace, some sleep.

Most of all I didn't want to see *him* again. *He* was the founder of our church, back for a visit in 1984, and I blamed him for what was happening to me now. He could—should have known what would happen. Perhaps he didn't care, not about me anyway.

Since his arrival I'd worked flat out to make sure that everything went smoothly on the practical level, and generally speaking I felt I'd done quite well. I'd had to learn a couple of very hard lessons about doing things on his terms instead of mine, but it was unbelievably exciting just watching him in action, and his presence on the night of my mother's death had healed one whole area of my life. Recently, though, I'd begun to realize something, and it troubled me constantly.

Other people who were close to him had changed. They were the same people, of course, but they seemed to be happier in some deep, quiet sense. They tended to say less, and when they did speak there was weight and assurance in what they said. They looked as if they felt loved—by him I mean. The simplest way to put it, I suppose, is that they were becoming more and more like him. They maddened me. Their kindness to me made me grit my teeth. I worked as hard, if not harder, than they did. I'd seen them hanging around him, talking, listening, laughing, whispering, often at times when there was work to be done. Nine times out of ten I would be the one who ended up doing whatever was needed, and after a while I refused offers of help when they did come. Their quiet smiles—their infuriating humility, it was all too much. Still, I did wonder . . . what about me? Would I ever change? Did he realize just how much work I did, and how much I would have liked to spend more time with him if I could be sure he wanted me? I began to feel bitter—lonely. I worked even harder.

Then, one Friday afternoon, the phone rang as I sat at my desk at home. It was one of the humble smilers, the kindest one. There had been a change of plan. Our founder had decided that he and his closest companions should go away for the weekend on a sort of retreat. I didn't think before replying.

'Fine,' I said briskly. 'When do we start?'

'Well, actually, he's asked me to say that you won't be needed this time. Just relax for a couple of days, you've been working hard.'

An icy calm enveloped me. 'Fine, fine, right, I will. Thanks—enjoy yourselves.'

I lowered the phone slowly onto its rest, and sat for nearly a minute, motionless, my hand still resting on the receiver. 'Won't be needed. . . .'

I rather relished the surge of rebellious anger that swept through me that Friday evening. It made me feel taller, more interesting, more confident. I paced around the house, smacking walls and making aggressive noises to an imaginary audience. Not needed, eh? I'd show them! The anger in me went to my head like wine. In the past I hadn't allowed myself to feel passion of any kind. It frightened me; it was like a bomb that would blow me to pieces if I let it. Now, for the first time, I felt released and hungry for sensation. Suddenly my imaginary audience was not enough. I wanted to go out into the night and feel like a real person in the real world. I grabbed a coat, checked my money, and slammed out of the front door. As I strode through the darkness, my hands deep in my coat pockets, my collar turned up round my ears, I felt like a character in a film. Each time a car passed I imagined the driver catching a glimpse in his head-lights of the tight-lipped stranger with the blazing eyes, and wishing, as he moved on towards some dingy corner of his mediocre existence, that he could be part of the wild, passionate world that this man must inhabit. Who was he, and where was he going?

He was going to the pub, and he was going to get drunk for the first time in his life. Only three pints, but that was two and a half more than I'd ever drunk before. My journey home that night was not easy. The pavement seemd to roll like the sea, and I had to concentrate hard on the problem of balance as successive waves threatened to tip me off my feet.

It was as I stood outside my front door, swaying gently and trying to work out a way to bring the key into contact with the lock, that someone spoke from behind my right shoulder.

'Are you all right, mister err. . . ?'

I turned round, steadied myself, and focused with difficulty on the face of the woman who had spoken. She had forgotten my name, and I had forgotten hers, but I knew who she was. She usually sat in the fourth row back, next to the wall, in our church, and she lived in one of the bungalows two roads down from me, and she was a bit older than me, and she wasn't married, and I'd sometimes wondered what it would be like to kiss her, but only in weak moments, because it was wrong and . . . why shouldn't I kiss her? I ached to kiss her. I'd never kissed any woman before, but I was going to now. It would be so sweet . . . so, so sweet. . . .

She gave a little scream as I put my hands on her shoulders and thrust my face towards her in what must have been a grotesque parody of kisses I had seen on films and television. She pushed my face away with both hands and ran terrified into the road and off in the direction of her home.

The discomfort of what I supposed must be a hangover on the following morning was as nothing compared with the sick terror I felt when I remembered what I'd done to that poor woman. I suppose some people might think it wasn't much, but set against what I claimed to be, appeared to be, and needed to be for the sake of my own self-respect, it was absolute disaster. Drunk and obnoxious, I had tried to sexually assault a member of the church. I, one of *his* closest associates; I, who had always had so much to say about self-control and discipline and character building. I must have been mad.

The following week was an endless bad dream. I sent notes out to say I was sick, and spent my time roaming the house, looking out of the front windows every now and then, expecting to see a policeman, or a group of stern-faced elders, or the woman herself with a posse of tough male supporters. Nobody came—I ignored the phone when it rang—and the tension increased. I hardly ate, I hardly slept, I wept over the realization that I hadn't a single friend whom I was prepared to trust with my problem. Nobody came, nobody cared—why stay?

Now, as I sat in the darkness of the hall next to my suitcases, waiting for morning, I felt a little better. Soon I would be gone, I would escape, and *he* couldn't stop me, even if he wanted to.

I must have dozed off because when I next looked up the first light of dawn was just beginning to whiten the glass panels in the front door. An instant later my body stiffened with apprehension. The silhouette—head and shoulders—of a man, had appeared in one of the panels. As slowly and quietly as I could, I rose to my feet, my eyes wide with fear, my hands clenching and unclenching with tension. As I turned, intending to retreat to the kitchen, the silence was shattered by an absolute rain of blows on the wooden part of the front door.

I knew it was him.

I clapped my hands over my ears, and shouted over the banging, 'Go away! Go away! I don't want you . . . please, just go away!'

The reply was a single thunderous crash on the door, and in that moment I remembered something.

'You can get in without me opening the door! You did it before—you did it when my mother died. Why don't—'

His voice interrupted me, tense with urgency.

'I can't come in this time unless you let me in.' His words seemed to fill the house. 'You must let me in!'

A further succession of crashes decided me. If he wanted to come in that much, nothing I said was going to make him go away, and I couldn't stand the noise any more. Fumblingly I undid the catch and drew back the bolt. As he put his hand on one of the glass panels to push the door open, panic erupted in me. I didn't want to have to talk to him about what had happened. I couldn't. Desperately, I caught the door as it swung open and tried to push it back, to shut him out. Instead, a glass panel smashed against his outstretched hand, and blood spattered over the inside of the door from a cut at the base of his palm. Horrified, I stumbled backwards towards the kitchen. He withdrew his injured hand and, pressing it tightly against his chest, closed the door behind him.

There were only two ways for me to go—up the stairs or out through the back door at the other end of the kitchen. I glanced over my shoulder and noticed something very odd. The back door was open—wide open. I knew I had locked and bolted it, but now. . . . There was someone in the kitchen; someone dark and difficult to distinguish was holding the door open for me. For some reason the prospect of passing that, whatever it was, was more terrifying than anything else. I turned and ran up the stairs into my bedroom, pushing the door shut behind me.

There was no fight left in me, no resistance at all. As I lay curled up on my bed, my face buried in my arms, I was as weak as a kitten, and as fearful as a child trapped between nightmares. This time there were no thunderous blows on the door, he just knocked gently. I heard the door open and close very quietly, then he was in the room and somewhere beside the bed. For several minutes there was silence. I couldn't even hear him breathing. When I finally risked a glance over my shoulder, I saw something I'd never seen before, something that caused the panic and tension to disappear as if by magic. He was weeping, not noisily or dramatically, but with the stillness and concentration that betokens deep feelings. But the thing that caused my heart to suddenly leap inside me with a shock of joy and total awareness, was the certain knowledge that he was weeping for *me*. Those tears, still welling up and rolling slowly down his face, were for me. For *me!*

I swung round and sat on the edge of the bed facing him as he knelt on the carpet, his injured hand pressed to his chest, his eyes, still brimming with tears, fixed steadily on mine. The boss, the king, the top man, was weeping over me, and everything was going to be all right—everything was going to be more than all right. He spoke, quietly but very clearly.

'You didn't understand. I fixed it for you. I fixed it all a long time ago. Getting drunk—the woman— jealousy—everything, they nailed me up for it, I bled for it.' He glanced at his injured hand. 'I'm still bleeding for you.'

There was silence for a few seconds.

'I love you,' he said simply. 'Do you believe me?'

I looked at the red stain spreading over the front

of his shirt, at his eyes, red-rimmed, tired, but full of warmth.

'I believe you.' The new happiness in me burst into a desire to do something—anything—for him.

'What do you want me to do? Let's go out and tell everyone what's happened. Or shall I get you a doctor? Oh, no, sorry, you wouldn't need a doctor would you, well what about. . . ?'

He laid a hand on my arm and smiled wearily. 'We'll sort everything out later. Right now, I'll settle for a cup of tea, okay?'

It was okay. Everything was okay.

## – 5 –

NOBODY HAD EVER confided in me before. Not surprising really—I wasn't the sort of person whom people tell their secrets to. Recently, though, something had changed. Since that strange night when I finally understood that I was loved, warts and all, by our church founder, I was somehow less stiff and difficult to approach, I suppose. I was glad about that, but I didn't seem to have any more answers than before, and right now I wished I'd got a few to offer the young man sitting opposite me, as he dabbed a tear away and sniffed miserably.

My visitor's name was Philip. He was about twenty, a good-looking chap, smartly dressed, but nothing out of the ordinary. He wasn't from our church. He belonged to a big lively fellowship on the other side of town, and at first I couldn't understand why he hadn't gone to one of his own church leaders or elders or whatever they called them over there. Later, I could see why he hadn't.

It took him a long time to get to the point. He'd seen me, he said, going around with our founder during the last couple of months, and he'd felt that I was—close to him. I'd 'got his ear' as it were. Having established this he said nothing for some time, just sat hunched in his chair, gazing at the carpet and breathing very slowly and deeply like one of those athletes you see on television getting ready to do the high jump or sprint or whatever. Now, I'm not a particularly sensitive sort of fellow, always likely to prompt in the dramatic pause, if you know what I mean, but even I could see that there was no point in pushing him, so I sat back and waited. At last his head lifted, his eyes, frightened but determined, looked straight into mine, and he burst into speech and tears at exactly the same moment. I caught the words as he sobbed them out.

'I'm not normal, I'm not normal!'

Over and over again he repeated the phrase, throwing the words out of him like someone baling a sinking boat. It was some minutes before he was calm enough to take a sip of water and tell me more clearly what he was talking about.

Philip's problem was that he only felt attracted to people of his own sex. He was a homosexual, or 'gay' as I'd heard such people called nowadays. He'd never told anyone—family, friends, people in the church, nobody. He'd never had a girlfriend, nor— he added—a boyfriend. I must confess I winced inwardly when he said that, and the 'wince' nearly reached my face. I was the first person he'd ever told, and as I sat facing him, trying to look relaxed, unshocked, wise and defensively heterosexual, it occurred to me that I was just about the last person on earth anyone in his right mind would have chosen for the job. I didn't know any other homosexuals, I didn't know anything about homosexuality, and I'd made a pretty poor job of sorting out my own sexuality, let alone anyone else's. I was quite a bit older than him and I'd never had a girlfriend either. Was *I* normal?

I was surprised, too, at the strength of the prejudice that must have been lodged in me. When I first understood what he was telling me about himself, certain thoughts popped into my head automatically. I'm not proud of them, but they happened. First, everything in me wanted to gabble something hastily to the effect that I wasn't like him. I was 'normal'. Then, when I was about to move my chair next to his and put my arm round his shoulders, I felt a sudden physical revulsion and fear and stayed where I was. My third, and perhaps most powerful response, was an inner determination to avoid the pain and tumult that was bound to occur if I faced my own sexual problems as he was doing. As I said, they're not very noble reactions, but they only lasted a second, and after a little thought I knew what I should say to Philip.

'Is it that you believe you can't be a Christian and a homosexual? Is that what bothers you most?'

Philip's gaze dropped to the carpet once more.

'I've been in meetings—Bible studies and things. They say it's one of the most . . . the main . . . it's in those lists in the Bible. You know, the lists of sins that stop you being—well—being a proper Christian.'

He looked up at me suddenly with the rather fanatical certainty of one whose convictions have been branded on him by the hot iron of guilt.

'It *is* wrong, you know. The way they talk . . . they sound so sure, so hard. I could never tell them, but. . . .'

The question—the desperate appeal in his voice and his eyes quite unnerved me. I leaned my head back and stared at the ceiling, just to escape the intensity of his need. I had no bright ideas at all, no special knowledge or expertise, no rights or wrongs, no thou shalts or thou shalt nots, no specific comfort or criticism. Perhaps I should have been better informed, I don't know. There was only one thing I was sure about. I could best help Philip by being completely honest. I leaned forwards, rested my elbows on my knees, and studied my interlocked fingers as I chose my words carefully.

'Philip, I'd love to be able to say that I know what you ought to do, but I can't because, frankly, I just don't. What I can do, though, is introduce you to him—if that's what you'd like. Mind you, I've absolutely no idea what he'll say or do. I only know that he'll sort it out one way or the other. Whether you'll like what he says. . . .'

An ember of hope flickered to life in his eyes.

'Would he talk to me? I mean, would it matter that I'm . . . like I am?'

Firm ground at last. I couldn't help smiling.

'It's never mattered that I'm like *I* am, Philip. I think you ought to give it a try.'

I waited.

'All right,' he said, 'when?'

I set it up for the following day. Philip was to come to our church in the early evening and see him in private for an hour or so. That evening I told our founder how nervous my new young friend was about the meeting. He hardly reacted. 'Wouldn't you be?' That was all he'd say.

The next day Philip arrived early, as I thought he might. I was already there when he walked through the front door. He was terrified. The poor chap was shaking like a leaf. He sat next to me on the front pew and wiped the palms of his hands on immaculately creased trousers.

'He's not here yet then?'

'Yes, he's round the back waiting for you. We've

got a little room there that we use for this sort of thing.'

I could have kicked myself.

'This sort of thing? Do you get a lot of queers coming along for treatment, then?'

There are limits, even to my stupidity. I didn't quite say, 'No, you're the first.' Nearly, but not quite.

'I'm sorry, Philip. I didn't mean that. I just meant—'

'All right, all right . . . it doesn't matter.'

He stood up.

'I don't think I can do this. What if he says. . . .?'

He stared into the distance for a moment, and then, as though someone had silently answered his unfinished question, he walked quickly towards the door that led to the back of the church.

'Through here?'

I nodded. He touched the handle, then turned back to me.

'By the way, I don't know if you think it was silly, but . . . I dropped a note in to one of our church elders on the way—to tell him what I'm doing. It seemed . . . I dunno . . . right somehow.'

I smiled, and nodded again. He opened the door, moved forwards, stopped, and turned to me yet again.

'By the way, I'm sorry about getting angry just now . . . sorry.'

I was getting rather good at smiling and nodding now. I must have come over as an amiable idiot, but at least I wasn't upsetting him. He opened his mouth again as if to say something else, changed his mind and went out, closing the door softly behind him. I flopped back in the pew with relief, expelling air noisily from my lungs. He was in the right place now. I could relax.

I must have dropped off, or at least dozed for a

time. A burst of throat-clearing brought me back to full consciousness. A man in a blue suit was standing in front of me. He was very broad, very distinguished looking. His voice was deep and confident.

'I'm sorry to disturb you,' he said. 'My name is Martin Sturgess.'

He smiled and extended his hand, obviously expecting an instant response. When I look blank, I look very, very blank. I got to my feet somehow, and tried to look intelligent.

'I'm sorry, I don't think we've—'

'Philip,' he interrupted. 'I'm one of the elders from Philip's church.'

He held out a folded piece of paper.

'He left this message earlier. I rather wish,' he added reproachfully, 'that he had consulted me before approaching . . . was it you first?'

'Me—yes, that's right.'

'And then, of course, our founder, whose time is as precious now as it was during his first visit. I can't help thinking. . . .'

My head was aching. It always did ache when I was woken suddenly.

'The thing is, Mr Sturgess, I think Philip was rather nervous about telling you.'

The strong, resonant voice broke in again.

'Scripture is quite clear in this matter. If Philip had confided in me, I would have explained clearly and in detail the course he needed to take.'

He paused, pondering visibly.

'Did you think we would condemn him? Did he say we would condemn him?'

I felt weak and foolish before this big man who spoke with such authority and assurance.

'Well, no, he didn't say that, Mr er. . . Sturgess. I think he just felt. . . .'

'Yes?'

'Well . . . look—can I ask you a question?'

'Of course—anything.'

'I just wondered *why* he didn't confide in you.'

It was his turn to look blank.

'I mean, I wonder what stopped him coming to you. Why didn't he trust anyone in his own church? I mean . . . why not?'

I trailed off rather lamely, remembering the time when I had hidden indoors for a week, unable to trust anyone with a problem that seemed larger than the universe. Poor Philip. Of course, like me, he did need someone to explain—clearly and in detail—the course he needed to take, but . . . he needed something else as well. He needed what I had found. He needed—

'Is he with our founder now?' Mr Sturgess interrupted my thoughts.

'Yes, at the back. They'll probably finish soon. Are you going to wait? You're very welcome.'

He stared at me for a moment then turned and took a few heavily thoughtful steps in the direction of the door. A little way down the centre aisle he stopped and swung round to face me again. His voice rang through the church.

'I am quite sure that when Philip returns in a moment, he will be aware of the seriousness of his position, and the need for proper guidance if he is to remain in the church. I do *not* condemn him. Scripture does not condemn him. Scripture condemns the sin, not the sinner. In the last hour Philip will have learned from the highest possible source that the true Christian no longer needs to sin, and he will need to learn to live in that truth until his faith is proved by the changes that take place in him.'

I don't know what I would have said in reply to this speech. Perhaps it was fortunate that Philip chose that moment to come back into the church. He checked for an instant on seeing Martin Sturgess, then walked up and joined us at the front of the church.

'Hello, Martin.'

The young man seemed quite relaxed now.

'Well, Philip?' The elder's voice was charged with anticipation. 'What did he say?'

I must confess I was agog with curiosity myself.

'He said he hoped he'd be here long enough to score a break of fifty on the snooker table.'

He noticed the puzzled frowns on our faces.

'I play a lot of snooker,' he explained.

Sturgess clearly thought this was deliberate flippancy. He took a step forwards.

'I don't mean that. You know what I mean. What did he say about . . . your problem?'

Philip's face became serious. He flushed very slightly.

'Oh, yes . . . that. Well, actually we only talked about that for a couple of minutes. He said it was very important that we get it sorted out. We're going to talk about it again next week . . . we're meeting again next week,' he added rather unnecessarily.

'A couple of minutes?' The big man's voice was incredulous. 'What did you talk about for an hour?'

The recollection brought a pleased smile to Philip's face.

'He asked me about myself. What I do, what I'm interested in—that sort of thing. He really seemed to want to know.'

Nobody spoke for a few seconds, then Philip looked at his watch.

'I'm afraid I have to be moving,' he said.

He shook my hand.

'Thanks.'

I think he meant it.

'See you tomorrow, Martin. I'll come round. We'll talk. Okay?'

'Okay,' replied Martin rather weakly, as the buoyant young man headed for the door.

Just before he went out he stopped and called back happily.

'Tell you what . . . I think he likes me! Cheerio.'

Poor old Martin wasn't looking quite so broad or so confident now. He sat heavily on the end of the nearest pew. After a pause, he looked up at me, and for the first time since we'd met, his smile managed to climb into his eyes.

'I wasn't wrong in what I said, was I?' He spoke very quietly.

I considered.

'Probably not,' I agreed.

'I wasn't right either, was I?'

'No . . . you weren't.'

'I see,' he said ruefully, and with great happiness I realized that he probably did.

## – 6 –

THE LAST PRIVATE goodbyes had been said. Today was the final day of our founder's visit, and twenty or thirty of us, those who had been closest to him, were gathered in the church room to hear him speak for the last time. As far as the rest of the world was concerned he had already gone; this was a sort of close family farewell. Now, thank God, I knew that I was part of that family, and I was more than happy to sit quietly at the back near the door.

I won't tell you what he said to me in our last proper conversation, but I will say that it took away most of the dread I'd been feeling about his going. How was he going? Where was he going? I didn't know. He didn't seem to hear me when I asked. He just said I should get people together in the church room that evening and put a glass of water next to a chair that wasn't liable to break as soon as he leaned back (he knew that most of our church furniture had seen better days!). I'd done all that, and there he was now, catching my eye over the heads of the others as he leaned back with an expression of mock fear on his face. The chair held, I'm pleased to say, and the buzz of conversation died away gradually until there was a complete hush in the room. For a time he said nothing, just gazed quietly at us with a strange mixture of pleasure and sadness. Finally, he sighed gently, straightened in his chair, and began to speak.

'Today I must go, but before I leave I want to talk to you for a little while about sin. Funny word "sin" isn't it? Old fashioned somehow. You do all know what sin is, don't you?'

He paused. The stillness that fell over the assembly suggested that we felt we might know what sin was. He went on.

'I certainly know what it is, not least because I had to fight it, just as some of you have fought it—or tried to. You know, during this visit some people have said to me—and I appreciate their honesty—"It's all right for you, you never sinned. You had it easy. You're the boss's son." A sort of divine nepotism I suppose they mean. Now, the people who say that have got a point in a way. I do love my father so much that it would be agony for me to hurt him, but—I want you to realize something, and I'd like you to explain it to others so that they understand as well. You tell them, when you feel the moment is right.'

His eyes, filled with memory, held us silent and waiting.

'You see, I had the capability, the opportunity, and the power, to *do* more, to *have* more, to indulge myself more than anyone else who's ever lived, or ever will live. One of your new translations of the Bible says that after I was baptized by my dear cousin, John, I had spirit unlimited. Right! Spirit unlimited—power unlimited. I tell you, I was bursting with it! I went off into the desert like a teenager wobbling away on a huge motorbike that he hasn't learned to control yet. Out there in the wilderness I had to learn how to handle all this power that was surging through me, and it was out there, where there was nothing, that I faced the fact that I could have anything and everything I wanted: women, money, possessions—the lot. They were all mine for the taking, and don't you believe anyone who says that I wasn't tempted, because I was. I felt every desire for every human indulgence that you do, and I fought it out, in the desert, on my own. That was part of the package you see—part of the whole arrangement—that I would face what you face, face it head on, see it for what it was, and choose to turn away from it if it was wrong. Not some of the time, not even most of the time, but on every single solitary occasion.'

His set face relaxed into a smile as an idea occurred to him.

'I'll tell you something that makes me laugh. Those pictures—you must have seen them—of me being tempted during the forty days and forty nights. I'm the tall cool-looking one with the whiter-than-white robe, dismissing temptation with a rather regal wave of the hand. Obviously you have seen that one.'

He joined in the general laughter, and after a sip of water from the glass beside him, continued quietly and seriously.

'Please don't believe it was like that. I roasted during the day and I froze at night. I was hungry, often thirsty, and always lonely. Most of the time I grovelled on the floor of the desert in a sort of sick daze, and all the time I knew that this incredible power pack inside me would give me everything I needed or wanted. Warmth, food, companionship of any kind I chose—all available whenever I wanted them, on the spot. I tell you the truth, I knew what one kind of eternity meant in that place. It seemed to go on for ever and ever and ever, but I didn't give in. Shall I tell you why I didn't give in? Shall I tell you what made me strong during those endless days and nights? It was love. Just that. Love.

'I loved my father more than anything in the world. I loved him with all my heart and soul and mind and strength, and I loved you, my fellow men—even then —as much as I loved myself. You see, my father had said, "Son, do it!" so I did it because I trusted him and I wanted to be obedient. Nevertheless, it took a long time to win that battle completely, but in the end I cracked it. I broke through to a point where I was totally one with God, wanting only what he wanted, seeing things the way he saw them, and ready to do anything he wanted me to do. Immediately—and this is typical of the way "head office" works—in came the angels with a packet of sandwiches and a change of underwear. You watch out for those angels by the way, they wear some funny disguises sometimes. I saw one the other day with a bottle of meths on Victoria Station, folding his dirty tattered old wings and trying to find a corner to settle in for the night.'

He was silent for a moment, looking at us as if we should say something at this point, but no one did. Later on at home, I read the last bit of the twenty-fifth chapter of Matthew's gospel, and began to understand it for the first time. He smiled wryly.

'See, I do know a bit about sin. I remember once, when I first came, I was sitting with my twelve lads and talking about the law—the law of Moses I mean. I think one or two of them were hoping that my message was going to be "anything goes folks". A sort of wild universal party presided over by an amiable old loon in the sky who didn't much care what people got up to. You should have seen their faces as I spelled out the house rules in detail. "Now," I said, "not only can you not kill, you're not allowed to want to kill—to feel the anger that wants to murder. Now, adultery, and the lust that leads to it, are sins of equal value. Now. . . ," and so on, and so on. They weren't happy, I can tell you. "Shifting from ham to ham" I think the expression is. At the end, dear old Peter takes me on one side and says, "I'm afraid I'm out of this, I'm not good enough. Does God really want us to be that good?"

'"Yes," I said, "He does."

'Long pause.

'"Well, I won't make it then, will I?"

'"No," I said, "You won't." Poor Peter looked so downcast at this that I went on to explain something to him, and I'd like to explain the same thing to you now.

'First, the most important thing is to do what God tells you to do. I'd told Peter to follow me, and that's what he was doing. I hadn't said, "Get yourself perfect, and then follow me." Just, "Follow me." The next thing was about the impossibility of ever being good enough for God. It was very important for Peter to know that God's demands are for nothing less than perfection. I wanted him to understand, later on, what my death meant for him, and how much I loved him, how far I was ready to go to fill the gap between what he was and what he needed to be, if he was ever going to meet the Father face to face. I'd like all of you to understand that as well.

'Let me try to make it clearer. Suppose you and I have known each other for years. You often visit my house, in fact I've given you a key so that you can come and go as you please. Now, over the years you've regularly stolen things from my home, some big, some small, some so trivial as to seem quite unimportant. I've never been to your house—you've never invited me—but one day you're sitting at home when there's a knock on the door. It's me, and I've come to have a show-down with you. Once inside I start to gather together all the things that belong to me, and stack them together in the middle of the room, right in front of you. Right through the house I go, opening cupboards, ransacking drawers, reaching under beds, and soon every little thing that you've ever pinched from me is piled on the floor between us. Finally, I reach over and take the biro from your top pocket and add it to the pile, despite your protests that it was borrowed and doesn't really count. So, there we stand by this mountain of stolen goods, and you're pretty troubled by now. What will I do? Police? Hit you, perhaps?

'"Did you steal all this stuff from me?"

'There's no point in denying it. "Yes," you mumble. "I'm sorry. What are you going to do?"

'"Forgive you. I just wanted you to know that *I* knew. Now we can start again."'

He looked searchingly at the faces ranged around the room, then spoke very softly.

'And I know all about each one of you too. I know what you've done, what you want, what hurts you, what you're afraid of. I know what you need. I know you because, in a way that's impossible to explain, I saw—I almost became each of you, during the three

187

hours that I spent dying all those years ago on that hill. You happened in me. You were punished in my body. The time I spent on that cross was a nightmare of congealed darkness and despair, a nightmare filled with selfishness, hate, murder, rape and filth of the most unbelievable kind, as well as apathy, ignorance and all your trivial unkindnesses that never seem to matter at the time. In those three hours I knew what it was to be an addict and a pusher, a torturer and a victim, how it felt to destroy and hurt and damage, and gloat over the agony of others. I knew it, I saw it, I felt it—and in the middle of it all I lost the one I was doing it for. He couldn't bear to look at me and I was so, so alone.'

Someone was crying quietly at the back of the room as he stood up and took a step towards us.

'There's a lot more I'd like to say to you, but I won't now. Just two things. Can I ask you to do something for me? Please, read the book. Get a version that suits you, one you can understand, and I promise you with all my heart that as you read it I'll meet you there, and we'll talk again. The other thing is the most important message I have for you. Look after each other. Forgive each other. Love each other. Don't hurt me. God bless you all and look after you until I'm able to come back again.'

After that he went very quickly. As he passed me he paused, smiled slightly, and said quietly, 'You've changed.'

'Yes.' That was all I could say. Then he was gone through the door into the darkness, and the visit was over.

# Choices

**by Jenny Cooke**

Life as a Christian is full of promise: the experience of joy now, and the hope of final victory over suffering. But what happens when a Christian loses his job, or remains childless, or has to care for a loved one until breaking point? And what difference does commitment to Christ make in the struggle against cancer?

In these and other instances – some from the past, some from today – Jenny Cooke traces the hand of a loving Father, testing the faith of his children and yet giving wisdom to make the right choice at the time of trial.

The challenge is there – and so are the rewards. Here on the canvas of real lives Jenny paints a picture of the fruit of obedience: faithfulness, courage and inner peace.

Kingsway Publications